Vanity Affair

Keira Lane

For You

Chapter 1

*I*t is a truth, never truly acknowledged, that a single woman in possession of exceptional fortune is in want of a husband. The unfavorable balance that has held women back, rendering them nothing but mere chattel and the presumptuous means to an end regarding prolonging humankind's existence, is tipping.

"Jane Austen would be proud," Eli muttered under his breath, pulling his bag open and throwing the beaten up copy of *Pride and Prejudice* in it. This classic literature class would be the death of him. The words, while wildly elaborate, bored him beyond reason. He knew after having looked at the syllabus, this section, Regency Era Authors, would be a slog.

"You sound thrilled, Ellington," Chase said, while he glanced around at all the empty chairs that surrounded them both. Chase sighed, shaking his head. "I just don't understand," he whispered.

Eli followed Chase's eyes. His heart sank at the realization. There was a distinctive radius of empty desks and stilted side eyes being shot in their direction. Students had avoided them. Eli gently elbowed Chase, hoping to break him out of the disheartened grief. "It's their loss. I've got the world's greatest best friend." Chase looked over at Eli, feigning a smile, packing up his things. Sadness brewed behind his weary eyes.

A small grin swept across Eli's face, and he attempted to redirect the negativity that plagued his friend. "Don't call me that, Chaunsey. You know how much I hate my full name," Eli teased.

Heavy fog lifted from Chase, as he couldn't miss an opportunity to razz his dearest friend. "Oh, come on, so your parents liked jazz a little too much. You can't blame them. His royal highness The Duke was an elegant persona."

"Pfft, elegant persona or not, I don't appreciate having such a ridiculous name."

"Stop being such an over dramatic diva," Chase said, lightness once again returning to his voice.

"Like you're one to talk, Chase. Or should I say 'Cindy'?" Chase's laugh filled the air, bringing profound joy to Eli.

"Hey, you leave my better half out of this." Chase's arms flew up in his best Vanna White pose. "She is a star and shall never be overly dramatic."

"Fair," said Eli with a small chuckle.

Chase and he had been friends since they were in diapers. When Chase had come out to him, there was an understandable fear that Eli would reject him. There was a special type of hate within their small southern community for those who not only identified as part of the LGBT community but also liked to dress in drag. It was asinine to him that people wound themselves up over how someone lived their life, especially when it didn't impact them in the least. He'd taken the time to read a few books on the subject and decided the best course of action was to behave like nothing had changed and, if he was being honest, he didn't feel like they had changed. Eli knew deep down Chase had preferences before he'd come out, but it never stopped him from wanting to hang out with his friend. He felt like an oddball in his own family. Everyone else was content in living a boring and ho-hum life, never questioning why they were going through the motions. Blind faith and a distorted reality plagued their tiny Atlanta suburb.

Both made the unspoken decision to remain seated until all the other students had filed out of the lecture hall, while blatantly ignoring hateful comments being lobbed towards them. They slung their packs over their shoulders, stood up, and synced their steps out of the auditorium door. "What are your plans tonight?"

"Well, I have to catch up reading this dull drivel and then spend the rest of the time wondering where I went wrong in life and why I need this course for an investigative journalism career."

"Again with the theatrics, Eli." Chase's eyes rolled so hard Eli thought they wouldn't circle back around and he'd have to make a visor in Geordi La Forge fashion.

"What are you doing tonight?"

"My grandma is dragging me to some sort of get together," Chase muttered.

"What kind of get together? Because it doesn't sound fun in the least."

"Apparently, the whole town is invited. Have you not heard about it?"

Eli furrowed his brow and tilted his head while searching the recesses of his mind for an answer to the question. "When did you find out about this?"

"I was told this morning. My grandma heard about it last night at her bridge group," Chase said, moving in front of Eli and walking backwards. "You should come tonight."

"I'll pass. Thanks though."

"It'll be better than reading a book written 185 years ago."

"This is true," Eli admitted, nodding. "What do you know about the hosts of the event?"

Chase halted in front of Eli and dropped his bag, looking around. The only living souls in the hallway were a handful of stragglers and them. Eli knew this meant there was a story, as Chase needed to have undivided attention and the use of his full body to tell it. "So you know that large house a few miles from my grandmother's?"

"Yeah. It's laid dormant pretty much our whole lives. I remember going on the property and mucking around the acreage."

"We had a blast climbing trees, playing Indiana Jones, that sort of stuff," Chase paused, taking a trip back to the past. "It's a wonder, looking back at it all, I didn't get in trouble for being there."

"Why would you get in trouble?" Eli asked.

Chase's smile faded from his face as he pressed his lips. "Trespassing."

"But we were kids. We'd have just been told not to be there, and that's it."

"A black kid trespassing on a white person's property?" Chase shook his head. "It would have been a significantly different outcome for me than it would have been for you."

Eli's eyes widened, realization settling in. He nodded in silent understanding. "So, tell me about this party," Eli said, breaking the solemn mood that had settled around them.

"Someone finally bought the place and I guess, to get to know their neighbors, the new owners invited families to attend a get together of sorts. It was in the paper this morning, too."

"I see. Are you going with your grandmother?"

"She demanded I show up, but is catching a ride with Barbara," Chase said, shaking his head. "I don't get why she keeps pushing me to attend social functions. It isn't like she's oblivious to the hell I've been through these last few years."

"Maybe it's her way of supporting you?"

"Support me? How so?"

"I guess, what I meant was that she doesn't want you to hide who you are," Eli said.

"While that might be the case, she's blatantly ignoring the toll on my mental and emotional health," Chase said. "It's like she doesn't take into account how it feels to be alienated by a community that, at one point, accepted me."

Chase needed support. "I'll go tonight. Can you pick me up? I'd rather not ride a bus for an hour to get there." Eli reached down, picked up Chase's backpack and handed it to him.

"Sure. I'll pick you up at seven," Chase said, swinging his backpack over his shoulder again, turning to walk towards the parking lot door.

"Sounds good. See you then."

Shrill yelling made Eli rethink walking the rest of the way up the sidewalk. He hated when his mother found it acceptable to spiral into a tizzy over trifling reasons. This was yet another episode of hers. Unwarranted and unwelcome. As soon as he walked into the house, he'd witness a bombardment of verbal diarrhea and get thrown into the mix, of that he was sure.

Eli let out an exasperated sigh, readjusted his book bag, and set his jaw before covering the rest of the distance. He had no sooner opened the door when his riled up younger brother, Lance, popped his head around, making him flinch.

"You're just-in-time, bro," Lance said with an ornery smirk.

"What sent mom into a tailspin?"

"Oh, the real question is, what doesn't send mom into tailspin?"

"That didn't answer my question, Lance," he said sharply.

"Geez, lighten up. Mom's upset because dad won't introduce himself to the newest residents of Meryton."

"Ah. I see." Eli raised his eyebrows. "I can't say I blame him."

Lance's mouth fell open at the sheer audacity of his brother's nonchalantness regarding the news. Surely he could see how exciting this was for the town. It'd been well over a decade since anyone new moved in. Eli saw the astonishment painted on Lance's face. Satisfied with the outcome, Eli pushed past Lance, who still held the knob of the door in his hand.

The small foyer opened up to the average-sized living room. Eli looked around to assess the state of affairs. James stood tall and resolute at the mantle, arms crossed in front of his chest, while Mark sat slouched in the wooden chair, feet propped up on the scratched and dented second hand coffee table, a hand rubbing his temple. Kit seemed to be the only one unphased by the current events. He sat reclined on the threadbare couch reading the comics from this past Sunday's Meryton Press paper.

"There you are," James' deep voice broke the silence. "Dad needs a bit of help. You know you're the only one who can smooth things over between them."

"I'm not sure why it always falls on me. Why can't any of you step up to the plate this time?"

"You know very well why," Mark muttered under his breath.

"It's not lost on us how you're favored by them both," Kit said, not bothering to look up from the splayed out colorful paper.

"No, Kit. That's where you're wrong. Mom favors James," Lance shouted from behind Eli.

"Oh, right, James will be the one who saves us all with his debonair looks," Kit muttered.

James' eyes zeroed in on Kit. Had he been Superman, Eli was sure the paper would have disintegrated from his glare alone. Luckily for Kit, the comic section protected him from the daggers being thrown.

"While you guys argue amongst yourselves, I'd like to say that we are all equal in the eyes of God, and so we should be kind."

"Oh, hush Mark. No one asked you to chime in," Lance zinged his brother's way.

"All of you shut up." Eli dropped his bag on the couch next to Kit. "You're giving me a headache."

Eli rapped on the heavy oak door. He knew his mom was a lost cause for the time being. She would be an emotional wreck until their dad went in and set things right. After years of mediating, Eli had learned the sure-fire way to get things resolved in any decent amount of time was to confront his father first.

"If you're coming to harangue me yet again, you can save yourself the time and effort, Jane" a weary but stern voice shouted through the door.

"Dad? It's me." Eli waited for a moment.

"Come in."

Eli opened the door and moved through the doorway before gently pulling the door shut. "What in the world is going on?"

"Well, I'm not bowing down or groveling to your mother."

Eli nodded, walking to his father's desk and sat in the faux leather-backed chair in front of it. "What is she wanting you to do?"

Henry let out an indignant snort. "She would like me to parade myself around—uninvited mind you— to the most recent addition to Meryton. And for what?" He paced the length of the room behind his desk. "This silly woman would have me make a fool of myself to assuage her fears."

"Fears? What is she worried about?"

"She seems to think that the only way to make sure you guys are set for life is to set you up with women who are better off than us." Henry sighed. "She worries about our financial ability to put all of you through college. I keep telling her we'll figure it out."

Eli hung his head. "Is the shop not doing well?"

"She's just trying to see you all married off to hedge bets." A defeated sigh escaped Henry. "I suppose, as your father, I should want those same things. It just grates my nerves that it seems to be her sole purpose in life these days. I think Lance's eighteenth birthday coming up in two weeks has sent her into hyper drive. She already sees Mark and Kit unable to attend college as a failure."

"Will you go visit these people?"

"I already did. I saw little choice. It comes down to me either looking like a fool or your mom living in such a state of unhappiness because of her anxiety, I'll play the fool every damned time."

If this was what marriage was, Eli didn't think he was cut out for it. Besides, he had more important dragons to slay, considering they put all their eggs in his basket regarding his furthered education. He furrowed his brows at the thought of the book in his backpack. "I suppose I'll go tell mom you did your best for her." He wondered if his dad had any idea this is what his life would come to when they got married. The stress of taking care of five children, managing a business, and everything else that comes along with life, had to be weighing both his parents down.

"Thank you," Henry said, as Eli got up and moved to the door. "Oh, Eli. Don't tell your mom why I humored her, please. She's stressed enough as is, and I'll never hear the end of it if you do."

Eli opened the door, a small smile spread across his face. His father understood his wife in a way many wouldn't have the patience to learn. He looked back, watching his dad as he sat in the tattered, rolling office chair, and wondered if his dad had been completely honest with him about the financial well-being of the store.

Chapter 2

S hattering glass echoed throughout the house, causing the flurry
of activity to halt. "What in god's name was that?" An authorita-
tive voice resonated from the kitchen. "I hope that's not what I think
it is." Heels clicked on the hardwood floor. *The runners should be here
by now. What time was it?*

"I'm sorry Ms. Bingley. It-it just slipped," the portly handyman
uttered, looking down at her from atop the ladder.

Charleigh peered down at the shattered crystal at her feet. She
kneeled down and picked up a large shard, rubbing the smooth side
with her thumb. Of all the times to have everything falling apart at the
seams. This was almost too much. "Darci!"

Stairs creaked as calculated footsteps moved down them. All eyes
shot toward the disturbance, watching the austere form with a prim
expression painted on her face move closer. With eyebrows raised and
her arms crossing her chest, she came to a halt on the last step. She
glowered at the chaos she found herself in the presence of.

"There you are! Darci, look at this mess. Please tell me everything will be okay," Charleigh begged. "I'm at my wit's end with this."

"Charleigh, this was your inane idea. I was against it from the start," Darci said flatly.

"Oh, drop the act, Darc. I get your disdain for all things festive, but this is a big deal to me." Rarely did she find her friend impossible, but today was not a good day for her to channel her inner tartness. "I have," she glanced down at her wrist, "five. Five hours to get the rest of this crap done before guests will arrive. I need my friend for this. Not a judge." The audible sigh that came in response let Charleigh know her friend had resigned to helping. Her shoulders fell, tension evaporating. She could do this with Darci's help.

"Hey, Char?" Her brother's voice carried through the open front door from the porch.

"What is it, Karl?" *Please let it not be something else going horribly wrong*, Charleigh willed over and over in her mind, hoping to take control of the uncontrollable and make it do her bidding.

"You probably want to come look at this?"

That didn't bode well. *Shit.* Charleigh peered over at Darci, who only returned the favor.

"You go, Charleigh. I'll handle this and be out shortly." Darci nodded toward the door.

Charleigh let out a sheepish smile, trying to hide the arm flail written all over her face. Glass crunched beneath her feet as she moved to meet her brother at the door. Karl held his arm out to her, helping her steady herself, a very welcome support for more than just balance. She stepped out onto the wooden wrap-around porch. At least the weather was deciding to behave. If there was one thing she knew about this place, it was that it could move from sunshine and warmth to overcast and snow in a single day.

"Karl, please tell me it isn't something terrible."

"Well, it depends on what your definition of terrible is."

"That doesn't make me feel any better," Charleigh said, grimacing.

"We're almost there."

"Wait. Does this have to do with the sign?"

"Maybe."

Anger bubbled to the surface. "What the hell happened, Karl?"

"How do you feel about Netherfield, rather than Nevanfeld?"

"Netherfield?"

"So, I might not have used my best handwriting when I went to the metalworker's shop." Karl rubbed his neck.

Charleigh couldn't find words. The only movement was the dropping of her jaw as they stopped in front of the large heavy gauge steel sign. There before her eyes was the most beautifully scrawled out wrong thing she'd ever seen. Charleigh could only glance between Karl and the sign.

"What was the fuss about, Kar—" Darci's voice drifted as she looked at the sign. "Wait. Wasn't this supposed to say Nevanfeld? As in Nevan 'saintly' and feld being 'field'."

A small squeak came from Charleigh.

"Well—"

"I knew I should have gone and done this myself," Darci said hotly.

"Now wait a minute. This could have happened to you too!" Karl shot back.

Darci scoffed. "Hardly. Words are my job."

"Netherfield sounds dumb," Charleigh cried out softly, wiping away tears that spilled over.

"We can fix this," Karl pleaded.

"Oh, we can, can we?" Darci muttered flatly.

"Yes, what about—?" Karl placed one hand on his hip, and the fingers of his other hand tapped on his lips as he thought. "What about if we add the word 'Park' to it?"

"Park?" Charleigh choked out.

"Yes, Park. Like the place kids go to play or people go for picnics." Karl's voice had gone up an octave in excitement.

"Park."

"Yes, Park."

"I quite like Park. What do you think, Darci?"

"Can I plead the fifth?"

"Fine. Okay, Karl. It won't be enough time for the metalworker to add the word Park to the sign, so you figure out how to fix this." Charleigh threw her hands up in defeat. "Netherfield Park. Whatever." She had so much left to still do. This was just one of the many hiccups in the day. She'd hoped to put her best foot forward. At this rate, she'd be lucky to put any foot forward.

The lukewarm shower did nothing to wash away Eli's heavy sense of dread. He wasn't one for parties, nor was he one for surrounding himself with idiots. A house party was the convergence of both. Eli had spent his youth avoiding those absurdities. He had better things to do with his life, after all. Damn Chase for entertaining the idea, and damn his family for going too.

After he had talked to his mother, they were told the expectations for tonight. It was bad enough that he had to go to this thing. Now he had to worry about the mockery that was his entire family. He would still go with Chase. Hopefully, arriving separate from his family would create enough of a distance from them so he wouldn't fall into the trap James would find himself in.

14

James, by far, had it the worst of them all. His gentle demeanor left him wide open to the manipulations and guilt trips of their mom. He didn't have the heart to upset her or tell her no, and she knew it. This allowed her to run amok with her master plan. James was agreeable, eager to please, intelligent, and soft-spoken. He was a good man and deserved better than what their mother was doing to him.

A knock on the door broke him from his thoughts. "Who is it?"

Kit's muffled voice made it impossible for Eli to understand everything he said, but knowing Kit and Lance, both impatient to the max, they needed the bathroom.

"I'll be out in five," Eli hollered. The joys of sharing one bathroom between seven humans. He couldn't wait to get out on his own.

The mild warmth he felt a moment ago, replaced itself with a chill after turning off the water which set the tone for the rest of the evening. He pushed back the curtain and grabbed the towel, wrapping it around him. The mirror captured his reflection as he stepped out. Eli glanced over, a disgruntled sigh, his only response.

"Come on, man! Hurry." Lance's irritation was clear.

Eli opened the door and pushed past Kit and Lance, who immediately rushed to be the first in the bathroom. The argument between them echoed down the hallway. He did his best to tune the noise out, hoping that closing his bedroom door would provide the silence he desperately needed.

"You look thrilled," James said, standing at the full-length mirror fashioning his tie.

"I've not had a moment's peace all day."

"You know, if you would just not wait until the very last minute to get ready, you wouldn't be stuck in the mayhem," James said, pointing his thumb over his shoulder toward the door.

"Yeah, I know." Eli fell on his bed, staring up at the ceiling.

"You act like this is the end of the world."

"James, I couldn't give a rat's ass about parties."

"I get it. You've big aspirations. New York Times."

"If it wasn't for Chase, I'd not think twice about staying put. What's the point of it? You know I hate small talk and people. Not to mention, folks in this damn suburb," Eli said, shrugging his shoulders.

"What about the people here?"

"James," Eli dead-panned with a pointed stare. "You know the reason that this is the first event we've been invited to in the last few years."

James nodded slowly. "Well, I don't profess to know much about, well, much. But I'd assume that living in a big city like New York, you're going to have to mix with various personality types and need to talk to people to gain interviews. No matter where you go, someone will not like you and there is no way to make everyone happy. Small talk and peopling is something you're just gonna have to get used to."

"Okay, where are you going with all of this?"

"I can see where something like this allows you to practice other skills a classroom can't teach you, is all." James tightened the tie and folded down his shirt collar. "I think it's about how one looks at this. It could be the worst thing there is, or it could be something to help you down the road. This won't be the last uncomfortable situation you'll find yourself in, Eli."

Eli's jaw clenched in stubborn determination. He was tired of it being about him and his perceived faults. "And what are you looking to get out of this, James?" Eli asked, turning the spotlight on his brother.

"Oh, you and I both know where my lot lies." James turned to make eye contact, a brilliant smile emphasized his dimples. "I'll stay here, marry, raise a family, and take over Dad's business. It falls on me to do these things and no one else."

"Are you happy with being forced into the obligation, though?" His brother's optimism grated on his nerves.

"Eli, happiness is what you make of it. It starts from within and radiates outward, affecting the rest of the things in your life from there." James walked over and grabbed his suit coat. He pushed one arm through, searching for the other armhole. "I'm happy just being here because I choose to be." James adjusted his coat lapel and shirt sleeves. "Anyway, it's almost seven. Best get your ass in gear. Chase will be here soon." James walked to the door, looked back while opening it. "Forget about yourself for a moment and think about the reason you're going tonight. It isn't about you right now, Eli."

A grunt was the only thing Eli managed in response as James walked out of the room and closed the door. James was right in more ways than one and he was easily Eli's superior in conscience and empathy. Now he sat alone with his thoughts, knowing he needed to reset his brain and consequently his mood before Chase showed up. James' parting words stung. Tonight wasn't about him, and he needed to remember that.

Chapter 3

C hase pulled up the circular drive, his mouth hanging wide open. Eli immediately felt out of his element. The beat up 1979 Toyota Corolla stuck out like a sore thumb among the more modern and sleek cars. Chase parked next to a shiny, black new C-5 Corvette. The stark class difference was unfathomable. They sat in silence, both looking around their surroundings before stepping out of the squeaky door sedan.

Gravel crunched beneath their shoes. The walk up was lit with twinkling lights, the glow dimly illuminating the path. Paper lanterns hung from tree branches, giving the walk an enchanted air with a soft, diffused glow. As they turned around the corner, the arrangement of lights, tulle, and glitter-covered sticks expressed an elegance beyond anything he'd ever seen. Eli stopped in his tracks. The pathway and exterior of the house looked to be straight out of a *Martha Stewart Living* magazine. This was unlike any house party he'd been to.

"Chase, I don't think I want to go in there," Eli said, uncertainty edging his tone.

"Why?"

Eli looked down at his sneakers and pulled at his blue jean jacket. "I'm severely underdressed."

"Oh, you'll be fine. It isn't like we've got reputations to protect."

"Fair," Eli said sullenly. "You look ten times better than me in your get-up, though."

"I look better than you any day of the week," Chase jeered, winking. "Besides, if I've the guts to do this, you can."

"A heads up just would have been nice."

"You said your family is coming, right?"

"Yeah."

"Didn't you pay attention to what they all wore and come to a conclusion on your own attire?"

"James was the only one ready by the time you got to the house, and he over-dresses for everything. Something about always putting his best foot forward." Eli ran his fingers through his hair. "If I followed his standards, I'd be wearing a suit every day to class."

"I see," Chase said, nodding. "At least you won't be unfashionably late. You'll be unfashionably on time." Eli rolled his eyes as Chase got a good laugh at his expense. Chase wore a fitted navy suit with a "splash of color" light champagne pink shirt and darker pink tie, topped off with a pair of brown cap-toe leather shoes. The soft light from the white glow of twinkle lights radiated off Chase's suit, painting him in an angelic glow.

He followed behind Chase, stopping when headlights broke the magic of the atmosphere. Eli turned, curious to see who the new arrivals were. The situation went from crappy to shitty real quick. The old clunker of a van pulled up in front of Eli and the front passenger window rolled down.

"Ellington Bennet! This. This is what you wore!"

Eli winced at his mother's ear-piercing loud declaration, unable to think of a retort as he was entirely at fault. He looked at Chase, his face filled with apology. "I don't want you entering alone. Can you give me a minute?" Chase nodded and leaned against the wall next to the house's front door. Eli walked down the stairs, getting close enough to hear his mother's continued scathing commentary.

"Henry, our son will be the death of me."

"I hardly believe that you will perish from sneakers and blue jeans. No, I think you'll survive this," his father chided, pulling forward to park.

Well, he'd done it now. There'd be no quiet entrance. He should have just gone in with Chase and ignored his mom. Eli let out a sigh, stuffed his hands in his pockets, and walked to the railing, leaning against it as he waited for his brothers.

Boisterous laughter announced Kit and Lance. Their feet hit the ground in quick repetition. They both barely fit in their suits from last Easter and a couple more months of growth would see their pants being made into high-waters. Lance brushed past Eli, completely ignoring him, set on prattling about the adornments scattered about. Mark wasn't far behind in his tweed old-timer suit. Instead of ignoring Eli, he stopped for a moment.

"Quite ostentatious," Mark stated, pushing his glasses back onto the bridge of his nose. He paused a second before giving Eli a nod and moved the rest of the way up the stairs.

James strode up, calm and collected. "Don't listen to Mom. You look fine. Come on." He nudged his head toward the house. "We'll do this together."

Eli turned toward the stairs and followed close behind James up the stairs. James gave Chase a friendly grin and a small nod, placing his hand on Chase's shoulder. The unspoken reassurance of his best friend meant the world to Eli. James had their back, and that was enough for both Chase and him.

Double wooden doors with decorative, colorful stain glass embellishments opened when James knocked, exposing a very different world than the three had ever seen. Stringed instruments filled the air with melodic harmonies. Evening gowns glistened in the ambient light, adding to the wonderment. Chase, James, and Eli found themselves unable to move. Each knew they were under-prepared for what was to happen.

"Welcome! Come on in," a bubbly voice broke their trance. "You are?"

James was the first to pull his eyes away from the festivities. Eli and Chase stood shoulder to shoulder behind James. They all found themselves face to face with a captivating enchantress.

"Um. Uh. I-Um," James bumbled about.

His brother, being rendered speechless, was a new one for Eli. A sharp elbow to his ribs jolted Eli into action. "He's James and I'm Eli Bennet. And this is Chase Lucas, my best friend."

A flush crept up her cheeks and she unleashed a dazzling smile that could knock Rocky off his feet, causing her celestial nose to scrunch up. Slight dimples appeared on either side of her lips, adding to her charm. Wisps of spun gold framed her rounded heart-shaped face. "Oh wonderful! I'm Charleigh Bingley!" She extended her small, manicured hand toward James, who gingerly took it. "It's a pleasure to meet you guys! Come on in and make yourselves comfortable. There are refreshments just over there." She pointed toward the arched formal dining room with her free hand. "And dancing is just down this hallway. Should you care for some air, the back doors attached to the living room are open and let out onto a deck!"

James, still bewildered, couldn't take his eyes off Charleigh as he moved past the door threshold, allowing Eli and Chase to file into the foyer. "Ms. Bingley, I hate to interrupt your hosting duties," a sheepish grin broke out, "but would you, err, do you dance?"

"Mr. Bennet, are you asking me to dance?" Charleigh asked, shutting the door behind them.

James glanced down at his toes for a moment before lifting his eyes to hers again. "It's just James. And yeah, I guess I am."

Eli had never seen this side of his brother. If he didn't know better, he'd say James was positively smitten. He looked over at Chase who responded with an amused grin and a small shrug.

"I would love to! Let me go tell Darci to watch the door for me. I'll be right back. Promise!"

As Charleigh walked off, smoothing her A-line satin and lace, navy, tea-length dress, Eli couldn't help but laugh. "We've only been here for three minutes, James."

James turned, looking back at both Chase and Eli, letting loose a small grin. "When you know, you know."

Eli's brow furrowed. "Know what?"

Chase's deep belly laugh echoed off the walls. "Come on, Eli. You're not that dense."

Before James could join in on Chase's ribbing of Eli, Charleigh was on her way back. Charleigh's friend was in deep contrast to her glowing aura and looked completely uninviting. Dark brunette hair was slicked back into a tight french twist, exposing her long, slender neck. The evergreen bodycon pencil dress with a scallop cut neckline and cap sleeves, mixed with the down turned tight lips put Eli on edge. He couldn't put his finger on why there was so much unpleasant rigidity to this woman. It was a party and she looked as if she'd rather be anywhere else, and if she was to take Charleigh's place in welcoming guests, Eli suspected anyone after their arrival would feel just as uneasy as he felt in that moment.

"James, Eli, Chase, I'd like to introduce you to Darci Williams, my best friend."

Eli reached out his hand in a peace offering. "Pleasure to meet you." He added a slight smile to help lighten the mood a bit.

Hazel eyes narrowed and judgingly darted all over him. She crossed her arms in front of her chest, refusing to meet him half-way and raised one of her arched eyebrows. "Charmed," she said, coolly.

"James, are you ready?" Charleigh asked, grimacing at Darci's lack of cordialness.

"Absolutely," James said, extending his hand out to Charleigh.

Hand in hand, they pushed through the crowd in the hallway and settled in the living room for their dance, leaving Eli to fend for himself. "So much for doing this together," Eli whispered under his breath to Chase.

Chase looked between Eli and Darci, and then to the food table. "Please excuse me," Chase said with a slight nod of his head. "I need to go find my grandmother."

Eli watched his friend walk through the archway to the front sitting room that was transformed into a decadent sprawl of hors d'oeuvres. A chocolate and champagne fountain topped off the elegant room's regality.

"Excuse me." Darci's eyes zeroed in on him. "Eli, was it? I'm going to need you to move yourself from in front of the door."

Eli's head snapped back to the sharp toned woman he'd been left with thanks to James and Chase bailing on him. He leveled a pointed glare. There wasn't one person in this world, well, outside of James and Chase, who could tell him what he needed to do. It triggered his deep-seated obstinate inclinations.

"Mmm, no thanks. Thanks though," Eli hissed.

"You're blocking the door," Darci gritted out through her teeth.

Eli glanced behind him before looking back at Darci. "I don't really think I am. There is easily a three to four-foot clearance," he said, crossing his arms and widening his stance.

Darci glared at him. "What the hell is wrong with you?"

As Eli opened his mouth to casually toss out a snarky rebuttal, muted voices making their way up the stairs outside stopped him. He pressed his lips together, biting his tongue. Darci rolled her eyes, turning to open the door. His parents stepped over the threshold.

"Welcome to Netherfield Park." Darci's countenance had changed at the drop of a hat. Where had the dreadful personality evaporated to? "I'm Darci Williams. And you are?"

His father, ever the gentleman, took his hat off and gave a slight bow. "Henry and Jane Bennet. Thank you for the invitation"

Darci glared at Eli for a split second before putting the facade back in place and looking at the Bennets. "The pleasure is ours. The lady of the house is preoccupied, but please come in and make yourselves comfortable."

Jane looked squarely into her son's eyes. "Oh, Ellington, remember your manners. I know I didn't raise you in a barn," Eli's mom huffed out before taking his dad's arm and striding off.

Darci watched Henry and Jane walk off into the crowd. "Ellington?"

"No. Eli," he dead-panned. "Well, it's been a real treat," Eli clapped his hands together, "but I'm off to find Chase."

Eli briskly walked off, not caring enough to look back. If he never saw that woman again, it would be too soon. He meandered through the front room, noting the people milling away from him. If he hadn't taken a shower, he'd wonder how badly he must smell to cause such a response. Chase was nowhere to be found in the house. Eli's eyes settled on the open french doors that led to the balcony. He pushed his way through the throng of idle bodies that lined the living room walls, stepping out onto the balcony.

"You found me. Where have you been," Chase asked in a small voice. The townspeople took great care to avoid them, which suited them both.

"Of course I found you. I'm sorry it took me so long to catch up with you. I got stuck with probably the least friendly person at this party. And considering the general disdain people have of us, that's saying a lot," Eli said while letting loose a nervous laugh.

"Got stuck?" Chase asked, raising an eyebrow. "You don't get stuck."

Sometimes Eli hated that Chase knew him so well. "Fine. I dug my feet in like an ass and refused to smile and nod my way out of an interaction."

"That sounds more like you. And who is the lucky person to witness you at your finest?" Eli crossed his arms over his chest and peered down at his shoes. "Eli?"

Eli sighed, putting his arms down and running a hand through his hair. "That Darci lady."

Chase turned to look into the house and focused on the figure who stood with one arm across her chest and the other resting on it, eyeing her nails. "You didn't," Chase replied exasperated. "You realize you're just making things harder on yourself, right," Chase stated, shaking his head.

"What do you mean," Eli asked.

Chase looked around at the dancing figures in the living room. The boisterous laughs mingled with the rhythmic hums of various pitch harmonies. "One day I'll learn to not hold my breath," he said, sadness rippled across his face, matching his tone. Chase let out a long sigh. "Eli, I've spent the entire time here being gawked at, avoided, and feeling the hate-filled glares on my back from people who I used to call friends all because of fears conjured up by political and media pundits," Chase said, while looking around the elaborate room disenchanted with the entire scene. "Just walking through the crowd and hearing whispered words like *avowed homosexual* and *homosexual agenda* regarding my *kind* wanting *special rights* and being carriers of the *gay plague* tells me all I need to know about the people of this town."

Eli's eyes drifted over to peer into the world that forbade Chase from being part of it. As he stood, allowing Chase's words to sink in, his eyes grew wide with understanding. "Privilege," Eli said quietly, looking back at his best friend. "That's what you meant by that."

A soft smile spread across Chase's face. "Yes. However, I also know you and your temper," Chase said with a chuckle. "I can only imagine what possessed you to turn your nose up at Darci."

"She's just grating," Eli spat out. "The air she carries herself in and the tone of her voice, all of it reeks of entitlement, which I don't care for. Not to mention she snubbed me when I attempted to shake her hand."

"Well, it's to be expected, I imagine."

"Expected? Who does she think she is? The Queen of England?" Eli huffed. "It isn't like she's an important fixture in either of our lives."

"Eli, you don't know who she is, do you?"

"No, why would I? Friend of that Charleigh lady?"

"The friend of that Charleigh lady is the senior executive of De Bourgh Publishing!"

"What the hell is De Bourgh Publishing?"

"De Bourgh Publishing is the largest romance publisher on this side of the pond."

"You've got to be kidding me," Eli said, bringing his hand up to rub the back of his neck.

"Nope," Chase said. "I learned about it from my old professor, Mrs. Delaney. She and I would chat after class about her author's journey. She's well versed in all things romance."

"Where are they based?"

"New York City."

"Of course they are. Fuck!" Eli grabbed handfuls of hair, pulling outward in frustration. "Chase," Eli's hands fell, covered his face before allowing his fingers to slide down his cheeks, processing what he'd done. There'd be no coming back from this level of screw-up. Why was he such an asshole? "I may have been short and a smidge snarky to her."

"Seriously!?" Chase was beside himself. His head involuntarily moved from side to side, refusing to believe what his ears heard, while crinkled lines littered his forehead. "You sure know how to dig a fine hole for yourself."

"How was I supposed to know who that was?"

"Eli," Chase said, taking a sip of the wine he'd neglected the whole time. "This is painful for even me."

"I don't know how to fix this."

"I don't think you can."

That wasn't what Eli wanted to hear. A hard slap sent Eli stumbling forward, almost smashing him into Chase.

"Boys, I'm in love!"

It took a moment for Eli to register what had happened, the sting on his back took its sweet time to go away. "Jesus, James. Why did you hit me so hard?" Eli attempted to rub the sore spot on the back of his shoulder.

"Sorry. I'm excited." The shrug that came with the apology annoyed Eli.

"Am I to assume that this lucky lady, who has spellbound you, is Charleigh, considering you've been dancing with her all night," Chase asked, never missing a beat.

"Yes! She is funny, smart..."

"Easy on the eyes, Darci's best friend." Chase shot Eli a chastising look.

This was less than ideal. Eli had insulted Charleigh's best friend, who James was taken with, and also pissed off the head of the biggest romance publisher. He not only had to clean up a mess because it would screw with his career, but now had to deal with his brother's happiness. There were two things Eli knew with no doubt: He'd judged a book by its cover. Publishers talk. Well, three things.

He was fucked.

Chapter 4

"Where the hell have you been?" Darci uttered under her breath, irritated.

"I'm sorry, Darc. I guess I just got carried away." Charleigh's eyes lingered upon the back of her great distraction.

"You left me here to deal with people. You know how much I hate people!"

"Well, I'm back now. Maybe if you lightened up and, you know, joined in the fun, you wouldn't be such a grump."

"You expect me to do what exactly?" Darci crossed her arms in front of her chest. She was not about to have any of what Charleigh seemed to suggest.

"Dance, Darci! There are so many wonderful people here to dance with."

"I'll certainly not. I find it loathsome when I'm not well acquainted with my partner."

"You're being unkind!"

"Am I?" Darci raised an eyebrow. "You've been hogging the only strong dancer all night."

"He truly is wonderful, isn't he?" Charleigh's exuberance at the oldest Bennet boy made Darci uneasy. Charleigh was always one to fall too hard, too fast. "You aren't being fair to the other gentlemen here, though." Charleigh craned her neck to peer through the crowd. "Look! There's one of the Bennet brothers standing just outside the back door with James and his friend Chase."

Darci leaned to the side for a better look at who she was talking about. "I don't think so."

"I can be a wingman for you."

Darci ignored Charleigh and kept her eyes trained on the man her friend was squawking about. It would appear she meant to hook her up with Ellington Bennet. She'd watched as his mere presence in a room seemed to disperse their party goers. He was someone she'd not like to acquaint herself with. She watched as Eli moved between James and Chase, making his way to the champagne fountain. Eli stopped for a moment, looking over the tables of food before grabbing a plate and filling it with meats, cheeses, and crackers.

Darci withdrew her eyes, peering back at Charleigh. "He might be fine to some, but he's not the type I'd choose to hitch my cart to." Darci sighed. "Look, I'm in no mood tonight. And honestly, I'm annoyed that you'd think I'd enjoy the company of people who seem to be slighted by their peers. Go back to your dance partner and stop wasting your time with me."

Charleigh looked at Darci with an incredulous glare. "Fine! Have it your way and be miserable," she huffed, stomping off toward James and Chase.

She glanced back over to where Eli had been, only to see him staring straight at her, a smirk plastered across his face. He lifted a pile of meat and ripped into it, chewing slowly while giving her a wink. Darci rolled her eyes and shook her head, watching as he turned around and sauntered back towards his brother, best friend, and Charleigh.

The car ride home was filled with silence. Chase and Eli both didn't seem in the mood to chat. Chase's eyes looked tired and Eli wasn't sure if it was emotional, physical, or mental exhaustion that kept him withdrawn, though it was probably all the above. As far as he was concerned, the silence was welcome since he was busy reliving every second of his encounter with Darci and the consequential slashing his ego took after overhearing her words to Charleigh. He'd tried to play it off, attempting to not ruin the evening for anyone. If he was being honest, she wasn't his type either, but it didn't keep the words from landing like an A-bomb on its intended target.

His brother's lit-up face flashed to his mind. He'd never seen James like that before. He was always so reserved in showing his genuine emotions, but not with Charleigh. She was different. The lightness and air brought out the very best in James. She would be good for him, if she would have him at all after the events of tonight. There was only one thing to do. He had to tell James what happened and prepare him to dodge any wreckage lobbed his way. Oh, and apologize. That last bit was important.

Chase pulled up to Eli's house. Eli looked at his friend, defeated.

"Look, it might not be as bad as you think it is."

"I appreciate your optimism, Chase, but you and I both know this is pretty bad."

"Well, don't give up hope just yet. It could be worse and might work out in the end."

"Thanks, Chase." Eli opened the car door and stepped out, turning around to look at Chase. "I'll see you at school Monday?"

"Yep. See you then."

Eli shut the car door and watched Chase's taillights disappear into the distance. He didn't want to be there. The last thing he wanted to do was enter through the front door and get bombarded with elation and excitement of the night from his brothers. Eli shoved his hands in his pocket and ambled up the sidewalk. There was no escaping this. He might as well hurry and get it over with so he could just go to sleep.

The door cracked open as he walked up. James peaked around the wooden barrier and smiled. "I've been waiting for you to make it back home!" His voice ended in an upswing.

So it began. "Hey, James." James opened the door wider for him to enter. "It seems like you had a great night." Eli attempted to end that with a reassuring smile but the concern lined on James' face let him know it fell short.

"Are you okay?"

"Yeah, just tired." He feigned a yawn.

"Oh, we can talk about things tomorrow." James' shoulders fell like deflated sails.

It was selfish to allow his hurt pride to steal the joy from James. No. He needed to be present for his brother, even if it was the last thing he wanted to do. "I'm fine. You and Charleigh seemed to hit it off tonight."

James perked up, his shoulders lifting as he rushed to shut the door. "Can I just say I think I have found the one?"

"You guys just met. How in the world have you found 'the one'?"

"It's a gut feeling. Charleigh is airy but grounded, fun yet serious." James brushed past Eli, who was still standing haphazardly in the foyer, and walked into the living room. "And she can dance," he said, while flinging himself on the couch. "Boy, can she dance."

Eli trailed behind his brother, hoping to get a contact high. Anything to help pull him out of the darkness he found himself in. It didn't work. "Okay, Romeo, I hate to drag you back to reality, but how on earth do you intend to win Juliet?"

"What do you mean?"

"Well, pointing out the obvious here, but we aren't exactly upper class. We run in completely different circles."

James' face sunk at the realization. He knew Eli was right. The chances that he would ever get to see Charleigh again were minimal, considering she was an Ivy League graduate and heir to her father's media empire, while he was just a high school graduate who stood to inherit his father's small hardware shop. "Yeah. You're right, Eli." James ran his hand down his face, attempting to rub the embarrassment from it. He'd lost his grip on the truth of their family's circumstances, instead letting the night carry him off on a cloud. He needed the attention to not be on him anymore. "So, what has you in the dumps, Eli?"

"I don't want to talk about it," Eli muttered. "I think I'm just going to go to bed. Forget tonight ever happened, or try anyway."

He didn't wait for James to respond before he turned and shuffled up the stairs to his room. As soon as the latch clicked, he leaned his back on his bedroom door, hoping it would reinforce him. His hands found their home in his hair, pulling the strands between his fingertips in frustration. He glanced around his room, catching despondent eyes staring him down in the mirror. If self-loathing were a bodied, living thing, it would be his best friend at that moment.

Eli needed a drink, something more than what he could find in the house. The window looked inviting, a beacon of freedom from these enclosing walls. He walked to the window, hoisted it up, and climbed out onto the lower story roof. This was his method of escape, especially when he didn't feel like seeing or talking to anyone in the house. Being one of five children had its perks, but also its drawbacks. There was always someone there, present.

He took a deep breath, exhaling while turning to shut his window. It was a ten-minute walk to the nearest hole in the wall joint that served liquor. Pete's wasn't his preferred place, but he didn't have it in him to walk the thirty minutes to The Woodshed. No, he'd have to settle on possibly contracting something from the railing and unknown stickiness on the bottom of his shoes in order to drink away his woes.

The breeze tousled his hair and crisp air filled his lungs. He found peace along the darkened roadway. His shoulders had lifted and squared in self-assurance by the time his hand grabbed the door handle. He needed relief and would give himself a brief pardon. Afterward, he'd come up with a plan to handle any fallout that might happen down the road from his actions tonight.

The thick scent of sweat and tobacco filled the air. A neon Bud Light sign flickered on the back wall, strobing the run down pool table in front of it. The long, patchwork wooden L-shaped bar held a few patrons wearing their trucker hats, plaid long sleeve shirts with puffy nylon vests over them. This bar definitely attracted a type.

"What can I do for you?" the bartender called out, while filling a pint glass with Miller draft.

"Well bourbon, on the rocks, three fingers," he yelled back. The latest Jed Aaron track blared in the background with all its twang glory. Eli took his jacket off, threw it on the straight-backed bar stool, and settled in for what was going to be a night of cheap forgetting.

The bartender placed a napkin down before putting the lowball glass on top of it. He turned to grab the Kentucky Gentleman sitting unloved on the bottom shelf of the wall, decorated with various other liquor bottles. Amber liquid splashed into the glass, stopping when it was about six ounces deep. "Tab?"

"No, thanks."

"Okay, that'll be nine bucks."

Eli pulled out his wallet from his back pocket, taking out a twenty and handing it to the portly fellow. "Keep six for you."

"Thanks." The bartender left, coming back a moment later to place a five-dollar bill in front of Eli.

Eli clasped the glass and took a hearty swig, only to find his nose on fire and his throat not faring much better. It took everything in him to swallow the oak turpentine tasting liquid down. His face stayed contorted for a few seconds after. "Well, this shit is terrible," he mumbled to himself, peering into the glass. It wouldn't be hard to nurse this, as he was having trouble finding the courage to take another swig.

He began going over the events of the party, allowing his disgrace to play on repeat. Why did he always seem to put his foot in his mouth? Eli raised the glass, blissfully unaware that he was on autopilot, and took another swig. Well, blissfully unaware until the burn hit his sinuses again. He cringed, giving his head a shake to correct the terrible wrong. It failed spectacularly.

The wooden door opened, allowing the night chill from outside to creep in, sending a shiver up his spine. He turned to look to see who the culprit was. "Fucking fantastic." Eli brought the glass to his lips and started chugging. He was going to need more alcohol.

Eli raised his glass, signaling a refill. The bartender nodded before turning his head to the customers. "I'll be right with you." He swiftly refilled the glass, setting the bottle down in front of Eli and walking to the end of the bar closest to the door. "What can I do for you ladies?"

"Hey there! We..."

"She," a strained voice corrected.

"I was wondering if you could help us. We..."

"She." An uncomfortable edge with a dash of annoyance was now present in the stilted voice.

"I'm looking for someone and was told they live nearby."

Eli knocked back his drink, reaching for the bottle to refill his glass himself. The sounds of heels signaled the movement of one invader toward him. He would pretend he heard nothing. If he didn't acknowledge or look over, maybe he'd avoid this whole situation.

"Eli?" The bubbly voice rang out over the music.

There was no way out of this now. Damn it. Eli looked up from his glass, turning his head a bit to make eye contact.

"Charleigh." He gave a slight nod to not seem too unfriendly. His qualms weren't with her, but squarely placed on her friend.

"Hey! We were, ummm," Charleigh bit her bottom lip, as she debated on what to say.

"In the area, touring the town," Darci stated matter-of-factly, coming to her friend's aid.

"Yeah!" Charleigh's face lit up, tension rolling off her shoulders.

"Darci," Eli said flatly.

Darci's eyes fixated on Eli. Her face was blank, no emotion to be had. It was unnerving to Eli. How could someone hide things so well they were impossible to read?

"Eli." Darci glanced around. "I wouldn't have thought this to be your preferred hang out spot."

"Yeah? What would be my hang out spot, then?" Eli quipped.

Darci's nose wrinkled up, her eyes calculated. "By your choice of clothes this evening: a house party."

Eli returned to his drink and took a gulp, refusing her bait. "So, why are you out at this hour of night, on a Friday, touring the town after having gone through considerable effort to throw an event like you did?"

"Don't you know how towns look and feel different at night, Eli?" Charleigh chimed in.

"I don't suppose I do. Then again, I've lived here my whole life and so it looks the same to me no matter the time of day or night." Eli took another drink, finishing the contents of the glass. His nose felt numb. Good. Shit was finally doing its job, albeit too late.

"Have you never left this town?" Charleigh said in utter shock.

"Nope." Eli put the glass down closer to the bartender's side of the bar and pulled out his wallet. "Now, if you'll excuse me, I need to be going." Eli pulled out another twenty, putting it with the five left on the bar. He turned to stand up but realized the two uninvited bodies pinned him in. "Can I please get by?"

Charleigh's face fell, and she moved back, allowing Eli space to get past them. "Eli, did I do something wrong?"

Fuck's sake. He didn't need to deal with any more drama right now and if he shared with her the truth of what was wrong that's all that it would be. Drama. Eli sighed. "No, Charleigh, you didn't." Eli took that moment to shoot a glance at Darci, who was staring him down.

"Okay. It just seems like you're trying to run away from us."

"No, I just need to get home. I have coursework waiting for me." Eli grabbed his jacket, slipping it on.

"Oh! You're at university?"

"Yeah."

"Does your brother James also go to school?" Charleigh asked inquisitively. "When we were sharing our life stories, he kept changing the topic to point the conversation back at me."

Eli really didn't feel like going through everything, and knew the more questions he answered, the more questions she'd ask. He ran his fingers through his hair, trying to piece together an answer in his fuzzy brain. "There's no need for him to go to school."

"Why's that?"

"He's taking over our dad's business when he retires."

"Oh! That's really cool."

"Yeah, I guess." Eli turned to face the door. It was so close and yet so far. All he wanted to do was stumble home and fall into bed.

"Are you able to drive?" Darci, ever the voice of reason, chided.

"It doesn't matter if I can or can't, seeing as I walked here."

Charleigh's eyes flashed to Darci. Eli knew that look. It was the look of being dragged into something he wanted no part of. "We can give you a ride!"

"No, I'm good, thanks."

"We insist," Darci muttered.

At least they seemed to be on the same wavelength of detesting each other's company and unwillingly in the same boat. Eli suspected Charleigh wanted to scope out where they lived and this was her ticket. For his brother's sake, he would play along. After this, though, he was done playing matchmaker.

"Alright. I suppose it would be nice to get back to my school work faster," Eli lied.

"Great!"

"After you, ladies." Eli jutted his arm out, pointing it at the door.

Five minutes in the car. He could do five minutes.

Chapter 5

"Eli!" Chase's voice rang out down the hallway. "Wait up." Eli readjusted his book bag on his shoulder, stopping in the middle of the hallway. "How was your weekend?" Chase asked, striding to catch up.

"It was fine. Nothing much happened," Eli said, shrugging. "I know Friday was hard for you. How are you feeling?"

"Eh, it's nothing I haven't dealt with before. It just takes a considerable amount of stamina and mental preparation for me to be immersed in an unwelcoming environment like that." Chase started walking, and Eli kept pace. "But back to you. You can't possibly give me that 'nothing much happened' bit. I've it on good authority that you had another run in, and not even on a different day—the same night!"

Eli hated living in a small town. Everyone knew everyone's business and liked to talk about it. It shouldn't have surprised him that Chase had heard something. He suspected he was the talk of the Sunday hens. They did like to cluck about the goings on.

"Who told you?"

"My grandma. I always meet her at Pearl's for lunch after church. Apparently, you were the focus of the conversation with all my grandmother's friends."

Eli threw his head back, closed his eyes, and shook his head in disbelief. "What did you hear and who did they hear it from?"

"Oh, nothing much. Just that Mrs. Barbara's grandson, Don, saw Charleigh and Darci in the crap hole bar near your house."

"Well, that says a lot about her grandson's character, doesn't it?"

"I don't see why it would. You were there, too, right?"

"But I'm not at church pretending to be something I'm not."

Chase fell silent.

Eli knew immediately the effect his words had. He'd been careless. His own confusion at why Chase practiced a religion that refused to accept him and instead damned him to roast in hell broke through. Though he was perplexed by Chase's beliefs, he was more so disgusted with how these same church goers were the ones judging Chase at school and at events like the one on Friday. Hypocrisy didn't sit well with him. So many that claimed to be religious seemed to only practice and adhere to the bits and pieces of their book that gave them free rein to judge and hate. As if they weren't guilty of being unscrupulous themselves. Eli wrapped his arm around his friend's shoulder and gave him a squeeze. "I'm sorry I hurt you."

"It's fine, Eli." Chase leaned his head on Eli's shoulder. "It's hard feeling like an outsider all the time."

"I can't imagine how that must feel." Eli's attempts to cheer Chase up weren't hitting hard enough. He knew he'd have to throw himself out in front of the bus. "So, Charleigh came into the bar trying to find where we live."

Chase's ears perked up, giving Eli a chuckle. "Oh, really? Why?"

Eli laughed. "I think she has a thing for James."

"Oh, that's glorious. Can you imagine little baby James' or Charleigh's running around?"

"The world isn't ready for that yet."

"Was Darci there to support her in her quest for fire?"

"Yeah, I did my best to avoid talking to her since I had already made an ass out of myself earlier that night."

"Smart move."

"I thought so."

They filtered into the lecture hall, finding their normal seats in the back. The first day, Chase had chosen their seats as if he was in a movie theater, in the center just far enough up to be away from the front and close enough to read the chalkboard. That immediately changed, however, when they realized our classmates had singled them out. From then on, they hid away, banishing themselves to the back of the room. More often than not, the floor was empty for Professor Fitzwilliam to pace unimpeded, but today, a single chair and a podium stood at the front.

"Did you hear anything about a guest speaker?" Eli asked while taking his *Pride & Prejudice* book out of his bag, along with the notebook and pen.

"No, I don't remember him saying we were to expect anything like that." Chase shrugged.

Professor Fitzwilliam walked in, dressed in a suit and carrying his briefcase. Something was going on because his teacher never wore a suit. He was one of the most laid back professors Eli had ever had, choosing to show up in cargo shorts, boat shoes, and a polo.

"Good morning, brains," Professor Fitzwilliam said, walking to his chalkboard, discarding his briefcase and picking up a piece of chalk. He scribbled on the board, set the chalk down, and walked to the front of the class. Seeing the scrawled out letters made Eli nauseous. "Today is unplanned, but special. We have a guest who is a senior exec of De Bourgh Publishing, and coincidentally my cousin. She's in town and humored my request to talk with you today about the publishing industry, as well as the literary opportunities out there for each of you."

Chase elbowed Eli in the ribs and whispered, "Professor Fitzwilliam's cousin?"

This nightmare seemed unending.

"I'd like to introduce my cousin, Darci Williams, who is in town from New York City."

The door at the base of the stairs opened and red soled high heels strode their way up to the small platform. Her hand was outstretched toward his professor. Watching his teacher beam, accept the hand and pull her in for a hug was the most confusing thing to witness. There was even a smile on her face. All he had witnessed was a bitter beer face frown, which he'd been positive was thanks to years of unhappiness.

"Thank you all for having me," Darci said.

The entire class ruptured in claps and cheers. Eli rapidly blinked in disbelief, taking in the reception she was getting. If only they knew what he knew about her, they'd be less inclined to cheer her being there. He sat, doodling in his notebook during the entirety of her lecture, spacing out. There was nothing he cared to hear, and he was sure what she had to say wouldn't enrich his life.

"Ellington Bennet."

Chase ribbed Eli again, breaking the daze he was in. "The professor called your name." Chase was trying to conceal the laugh. "Go up there."

"What did I miss?"

"You're about to find out." Chase burst into deep giggles, tears welling up in his eyes.

Eli raised out of his seat and moved down the stairs toward where his teacher stood. Professor Fitzwilliam's face was full of joy, like a bird watching one of their babies take off flying from the nest for the first time. "I'm so proud of you, Eli. You've worked hard to get to this point."

He looked back into the crowd to find his friend laughing his ass off. He still didn't know what was happening. Darci walked over to him and extended her hand. Eli's eyes grew as wide as the realization settled in. He had to shake hands with her. That was the last thing he wanted to do. Eli forced down the embarrassment he felt and took her hand in his, shaking firmly. His eyes bore into hers. A silent discussion passed between them, while everything else around them fell away.

"Now, Eli," his professor continued, "I don't want you to worry at all about the course work for the rest of the year. This internship with De Bourgh will count toward your credit for this course."

An internship? At De Bourgh? What the absolute hell just happened? Eli couldn't wait to run offstage and disappear. What would he do with an internship at a publishing house with no ties to journalism? This internship was directly at odds with his career path. He wanted to travel the world and to war-torn countries, not read a bunch of verbal flim-flam that women read to make up for their sad love lives. This was, of course, in addition to having to work under Darci Williams.

Everyone in the class quieted down, and Professor Fitzwilliam signaled for Eli to go back and have a seat before continuing. "This is a tremendous opportunity. Thank you dear cousin, for taking time out of your day to come educate my students."

"The pleasure was all mine, Fitz. I enjoyed my time here." Darci looked out over the crowd, her eyes settling on Eli. "You all have bright futures ahead of you, and the fact you are sitting in this class today speaks volumes to your character."

"Smolder alert," Chase said, as Eli took his seat once again.

Eli ignored him, meeting Darci's eyes and holding her gaze. She would not intimidate him.

Darci waited for the class to finish emptying before confronting her cousin. She hadn't known the top student of the class would be Eli Bennet. Hell, she didn't even know he was in this class. It took everything in her to stay composed when his name had been called out. There was something about him that grated on her. He was brazen and crass. How would she explain this to Keats? This was now her reputation on the line, and she didn't care for it. "Fitzwilliam!"

Her cousin turned toward her wide-eyed. "What?"

"How come you didn't tell me Ellington Bennet was your top of class?"

"Why does it matter? You'd already told me to give the student that performed the best the internship."

"Why? He is incorrigible," Darci huffed.

"Look, Eli is a brilliant student and would be a great asset to De Bourgh Publishing."

"Keats will have my head."

"Keats is a stodgy old curmudgeon. You and I both know that."

"Not the point."

"You need new life breathed into the company, and who better to do it than someone so far removed they wouldn't know a thing about the romance industry?" Fitz walked to the chalkboard, bending to pick up his briefcase. "That was your intention, was it not? To find innovative ideas?"

She hated her words being thrown back into her face. Fitz's smirk told her what she already knew. He had won. This was how it was going to be, like it or not. It was now time to make the best of the situation.

Darci called out to Fitz, stopping him as he held the door open. "Will you tell him the expectations and information detailing the contract and travel?"

"No, Darc. I think I'll leave that up to you." Fitz moved through the open doorway in a fit of laughter.

The echo of the door shutting was the only comfort Darci had. What was she to do? God help De Bourgh and while he was at it, her.

Chapter 6

The party, the bar, and now his school. No where was safe in this cursed place. Fate was out to get him, and he couldn't fathom the reasoning behind it. He'd not left a room so quickly before. He didn't even wait for Chase to gather his things. Air and space were what he needed.

Rye moved in the breeze, reminiscent of rolling waves. The field was the only place he could think to go where he'd be safe from questioning minds. It was also the last place on earth he would expect to find Darci. He couldn't help but feel that they were being thrown together by an unnatural force. A force that he wished would fuck off already.

Not taking the bus allowed him to take the long way home. He needed the time to process what had happened. There were far better qualified people to fill this internship spot. Several were taking the course with the aspiration to work in publishing, and he wasn't one of those.

Though the opportunity would thrill his parents. There was no doubt in his mind that they would think this to be the leg up in the literary world he needed to make his dreams come true. They, however, lacked the background information on why this was a terrible thing. Maybe talking to his mom would be good for him. Then again, this could send her into a panic. It really was a crap shoot. James. He needed to talk to James. If anyone could see it from both sides and knew the history there, it was him.

Eli turned on his street and immediately felt the pull to turn around and run away. Charleigh's car was in front of their house. Fuck. His hands flew to his head as he looked for something to kick. With nothing in sight for his feet to demolish, he turned to the telephone pole that was nearby and moved in, punching it repeatedly with his fists. The old, partially rotted wood creaked with each crushing blow. Pain radiated from his fingers and knuckles. Blood running down his fingertips wasn't enough to break him from his rage filled assault. Maybe if all he could see wasn't red, he'd have seen the glimmer of sunlight reflecting off his hand's next target. His skin caught on something as he pulled his hand back. Blind rage dissipated, as his eyes fell on the bloodied metal nail.

"Damn it!" Eli let out in a guttural scream. He looked down at his right hand, trying to see how bad the cut was, hoping to god it wouldn't need stitches. Obviously, punching the crap out of a stationary log wasn't among the best decisions of the day. If he was being honest, none of the decisions he had made the last couple of weeks were any better.

He let out a sigh and trudged, defeated, toward the fate that awaited him. First thing was first, he needed to get his hand cleaned up. Eli walked through the front door, bypassing his mother, brothers, and the regal guests sitting on their secondhand couch. Eye contact was definitely something he didn't want to make.

"Eli? Eli!" his mother's shrill voice yelled after him.

Nope. Just keep walking. He made a beeline to the kitchen, pulling the first aid kit out from under the sink. It took him a minute to open the box with his non-dominant hand and sort through to find the alcohol wipes, iodine pads, and bandages. Footsteps fell behind him.

"Dear god, Eli," James' voice wavered a bit. Blood wasn't his thing. He'd pass out if Eli allowed him to see his hand in that state.

"Go away, James," Eli said through a wince, as he had opened one of the alcohol wipes and applied it to his bloodied knuckles and fingers.

The thudding of more footsteps in rapid succession informed Eli he was about to have a full audience.

"Oh, my sweet baby! What have you done to yourself?" Fear flooded his mother's voice.

"Mom, I'm fine."

"You are not fine! You need to go to the hospital." Her face turned white when she saw the blood dripping in the kitchen sink and on the counter. "I don't know what to do. Your father has the van right now."

Charleigh stood on her tippy toes, looking over his mother's shoulder. "Yeah, Eli. That looks pretty bad. I can take you to the hospital. It looks like it might need stitches."

He couldn't get the bleeding to slow down. Maybe Charleigh was right, though he hated to cause a financial burden on his family because of his lack of control. Out of his peripheral vision, he saw Darci move around the crowd. She'd been lurking in the back, no doubt elated by his stupidity. To his surprise, she'd donned a pair of jeans, a sweater, and Keds.

"Let me look at that." The sound of her firm voice quieted the room down.

Eli didn't know how to respond, so he jutted his hand out toward Darci. She took it, gently turning it, taking in every angle.

"I don't think he needs the hospital." Darci released his hand, turning to his mother. "Mrs. Bennet, do you have a rag you don't mind ruining?"

"I do! I'll go grab it."

"Eli, go sit at the table," Darci said.

He had been attempting to read her face, trying to find any emotion as she executed the commands. It was fruitless. She was a stone golem. "Okay." Eli turned, walked to the table, pulled out a chair, and sat down.

Darci grabbed the first aid kit from the kitchen counter and brought it to the table with her, taking a seat opposite Eli. She began pulling items out methodically and laid them on the table in front of her. Jane barreled around the corner with an old dish towel she'd pulled from the linen closet. "Thank you, Mrs. Bennet," Darci said, taking the towel.

"My pleasure! Oh, I hope he'll be alright."

James put his hand on his mother's shoulder, gently tugging her away from the scene. "Come on, Mom. Let's go back into the living room. It seems he's in very capable hands with Ms. Williams." His mother nodded in agreement, pivoting to follow Charleigh and James out of the kitchen.

Darci worked quickly, wrapping his hand in the towel and applying pressure. Her hands were agile and firm, though capable and soft. She moved like he'd seen nurses do, tending to their patients.

Eli cleared his throat. "You look like you do this often."

"What?"

"The whole fixing people up thing."

"Oh. No."

The awkward silence lingered. Eli didn't want to put forth the effort, but he knew he needed to try. Like it or not, the internship saddled them together for the foreseeable future. He tried again. "I appreciate you doing this. It wasn't necessary, though I was having a helluva time doing it myself."

"No problem."

How the hell did this woman not see him trying? Least she could do is give him something, anything, to work with, instead of consistently shutting him down. Darci took the towel off his hand and looked at the wounds. The bleeding had stopped with the pressure applied. It didn't look as bad as he'd thought it would be. Bits of skin stuck up, having met the rough wood an unknown amount of times.

"I'll need to clean the wound." Darci reached into the kit, pulling out the tweezers. Her eyes squinted. "What did you punch that was wooden?"

"What are you talking about? I didn't punch wood," he lied.

Darci looked up at Eli. There it was. Her forehead wrinkles and the raising of her right eyebrow said it all. She held up the tweezers that clutched a splinter, calling bullshit. What a fantastic first facial expression to get. Eli sighed. He might as well hit this head on.

With a roll of his eyes, Eli responded to the silent call out. "It was a telephone pole."

"A telephone pole?"

"Yes. A telephone pole."

"Why would you do something so dumb?" Darci asked, as she continued removing thin splinters of wood from the flat of his fist. Eli glared at Darci in response. They spent the rest of the time in deafening silence.

Sounds of shoes slapping the pavement and loud bickering voices announced Eli's younger brothers. He looked at Darci, who was standing next to the fireplace looking over the surroundings like a hawk watching potential prey. The chaos that was about to bound through the door set Eli's nerves on edge. He was already in a predicament regarding his own character and to suffer further embarrassment, thanks to his tactless siblings, was shit icing on the shit cake.

Lance bolted through the door first with Kit pushing his way through, nearly stumbling and falling over Lance. Mark gingerly followed, rolling his eyes. As soon as their eyes met Darci's, they stopped in their tracks, straightening their posture. Lance clutched a copy of the Meryton Press in his hand.

James cleared his throat. "Charleigh and Darci, you remember my younger brothers from the party, Lance, Kit, and Mark."

Charleigh jumped from her seat and ran over to Lance, holding out her hand. "I do. Pleasure to meet you all again."

Lance took her hand dramatically, bending down to kiss the back of it. "It's our pleasure."

James stared daggers at Lance, irritation painted thickly upon his face. It seemed they hit their target as Lance looked over and winced, furrowed his brow, and pulled his lips tight. He knew he had overstepped.

"Oh, heavens." Charleigh chuckled at the overboard reaction.

Kit stepped up, eyes focused on Darci. Eli saw what was to come, and he couldn't stop it. "Ms. Williams, is it true that you make $500,000 a year?"

Darci's eyes zeroed in on Kit. Eli's mouth dropped open, and he wished the chair he was sitting in would shroud him. James, in panic, inhaled so hard and fast that he started coughing, choking on his spit. Lance looked at the back of Kit's head, his eyes wide as saucers. Mark, who stood behind Lance, took several steps backward, looking ready to bolt at a moment's notice. The color had drained from Mrs. Bennet's face. Charleigh, wedged between Lance and Kit, didn't take her eyes off Lance. Not a soul dared move or even breathe.

Jane pursed her lips, squinted her eyes, and shook her head, silently censuring Kit. "My deepest apologies, Ms. Williams. My son apparently lacks manners and common sense." She turned to look at Darci, who was still dead set on her original target. "I can promise you that this behavior will stop immediately. Isn't that right, Kristopher Bennet?"

Kit's eyes fell to the floor, his face flushed. "Yes, ma'am. I'm sorry, Ms. Williams." His voice dropped in decibel at the tail end.

Darci's eyes narrowed. "Eli, can I talk to you in private?"

Fuck. He dare not ask what else could go wrong.

"You can use your father's study, Eli," his mother chirped.

Eli nodded in his mother's direction. "Follow me." He hoped his tone didn't reflect the disdain for what was about to happen.

Antiquated floorboards creaked under their feet as Eli led them down the hallway to the study. His fate hung in the balance, and the boat was more than rocking. It was about to capsize with him in it. Eli paused in front of the dinged up door. The cold of the doorknob that protruded from its perch was a welcome relief to his swollen hand. Door hinges groaned, seemingly in agreement with how he felt internally. Eli stepped aside, allowing Darci to move past him. Her hair swept by him, the fragrant sweet aroma of floral perfume wafted up and filled his senses. He hated to admit it, but she smelled good.

Darci moved further into the room, wandering around to look at his father's collection of books and knickknacks. He couldn't take his eyes off of her. She was so far out of her element; it reminded him of Blane seeing Andie's house for the first time in that *Pretty in Pink* movie. Stark contrasts; his world and hers. Eli turned to close the door. When the latch clicked shut, Darci looked up from the copy of *The Scarlet Letter* she'd grabbed. She pivoted to set the book back down and walked toward Eli. By the time Eli had spun around, Darci was a foot away. His eyes met hers, and he licked his lips. He was aware of the signal that he might have been sending, but his throat was scratchy and his mouth dry, like he'd filled it full of cotton balls.

"So, about today," Darci said, breaking the silence..

Eli rubbed the back of his neck with his good hand before shoving it in his pocket. "What part of today?" He didn't mean to sound difficult, but a lot of *terribles* had happened, and he wasn't sure which she was referring to.

A sincere, hearty laugh escaped Darci, surprising Eli. "I meant the scholarship with De Bourgh Publishing," Darci said with a small chuckle.

"Oh, right, I'm going to be honest with you. This opportunity is wonderful for someone out there that isn't me. It won't do much to propel my career."

Calm seeped from her face as quickly as it had appeared. "I'm sorry. What?"

"I see no way a romance publisher is going to do anything for me."

"You can't be serious."

"Oh, I very much am." Eli crossed his arms over his chest in response, widening his stance.

Darci set her jaw in defiance. She wasn't used to people turning her down. In fact, it was the other way around. People begged her for job opportunities. "Wow. You're positively foolhardy."

"Excuse me?" Eli dropped his arms to his side, his eyes narrowing.

Darci looked around the library and back at Eli. "You've a chance to make something of yourself, and you're turning it down."

"Make something of myself? Who are you to tell me I'm not already something?" Eli had held back long enough. It was time she knew just what he thought of her. "I don't enjoy having someone insult me or my family nor do I enjoy people who behave in a pompous way. I'll do just fine without your help as I've made it this far without you."

Darci's mouth hung slack jawed. "I can see we are ill-fitted to work together. Thank you for your time." Darci pushed past Eli, opened the door and stormed out. Eli's shoulders slumped.

She seemed to always bring the worst out in Eli. He waited for the thud of the front door before coming out of the study and walking through the living room to seek solace in his room.

"Oh, Eli! You didn't hear," Lance shouted from the couch he was lying on.

"Lance, I can't take anymore news, good or bad, today."

Kit chimed in. "It's nothing important. Charleigh told us that Meryton is hosting a Halloween Masquerade on the 31st before they left."

Eli rolled his eyes and stalked off. Their lives revolved around parties while his life was falling apart faster than he could tape it back together.

Chapter 7

Flickers of light emitted from the wrought iron candelabras, casting shadows upon the velvet deep red drapes. The chill from the night hung in the air in the puffs of gray swirling vapor. A stringed quartet filled the atmosphere with the rich melodic tones of Aram Khachaturian's "Masquerade Waltz". Meryton's library had transformed for the night to a lavished Baroque fantasy. Light danced on the twisted columns that rose, getting lost in the vaulted unlit depths.

Eli adjusted his homemade paper mache *Phantom of the Opera* style mask. He and Chase had been debating on even attending, but they both agreed that the allure of something he probably wouldn't experience again in his life won out. Not to mention, this gave them an opportunity to actually blend in for once.

The theme, which was entirely appropriate for the venue of the ball, was literary works. It pained him to take his only copy of *The Count of Monte Cristo* and tear it to shreds, using the pages to form his mask. The red checkered design was simple enough, with the remaining unpainted pieces showing the words from the torn pages.

His hand found his right cufflink and tugged it, making sure it was firmly in place. He'd catch no small amount of grief if he lost one of his grandfather's heirlooms passed down to him. Eli pulled gently at the red tie around his neck that stifled him.

James walked up beside him, lingering in the middle of the arched walkway. He'd chosen to wear a half mask, decorating it in deep blues and silver. "You clean up nice." James threw his arm around Eli's neck.

"Thanks."

"Where'd you find the suit?"

"I stole it from some guy I know that likes to wear these things daily."

James laughed. "You're welcome. I'm glad someone can use it, now that it no longer fits me." He studied Eli's mask. "Your costume is fantastic. It'd shock me if you don't catch a few eyes tonight. Where's Chase?"

"What gives you the impression I look to catch any eyes? And he said he would be a little late getting here."

"Ah, okay. So you want to be single for the rest of your life?"

"No, but I have standards."

"And what would those be?"

"Someone who I can have an intellectual conversation with and doesn't bore me to tears."

"Well, good luck finding someone like that who'll also put up with your ass," James teased before walking off, leaving Eli to dwell on his lackluster love life.

Murmurs from the throng of guests inundated Eli, overstimulating his senses. He felt out of place and alone. The masks added to the cacophony of sensory overwhelm since he couldn't see who anyone was. Anxiety bubbled up, his chest constricting. It'd been only five minutes since they'd arrived, and he already wanted to leave. Laughter rang out behind him, forcing him further into the building, to move out of the new arrivals way. He needed to find a corner not already occupied to hide until Chase made it there.

Eli pushed his way through the crowded room. Women in low-cut, elaborate gowns created a formidable barrier. Virago sleeves swept against his shoulders, the wearer's faces hidden from view. As the last note rang out from the violins, attendees directed their attention to the platform the musicians sat upon, earnestly waiting to hear what the next song would be. Violinists began plucking their strings for the first measure, ushering in the cellist's first resonating bow stroke, solidifying the tempo for *Glycerine* by Bush.

Disguised men wandered about, bowing in front of hopeful partners. Some took the hands of ornately dressed regality, leading them further into the room. Others, upon rejection, disappeared, slinking off to lick their wounds. Eli scanned the chaos before him. There was no way he'd be dancing tonight. No, he'd be happy soaking in the ambience unnoticed. A pillar at the far wall stood vacant. It would make for a fine perch where he could be fully content with observing. He kept his head down, taking care to avoid stepping on dress hems. The kaleidoscope of color painted his journey to the furthest reaches of the room.

Eli collided with a solid form. His breath caught in his chest, and his stomach fluttered at the sight of the dark red figure that stood in front of him. He tilted his head as he took her in. Her gown differed from the others, standing out for being rather simple. There were no patterns to it, the lace being its only embellishment. Her perfectly outlined collarbones and neck beckoned to be kissed. A modest heart-shaped diamond pendant lay squarely in the center of her lower neck; her dark brown hair swept up in a loose updo. Red and black hearts adorned with gemstones decorated her half mask.

"Pardon me," Eli breathed out.

Bright eyes shown, a smile creeping up on the heavenly face. She took a step closer to Eli, her eyes studying him for a moment. "*The Count of Monte Cristo*?"

Eli grinned widely, nodding. "Queen of Hearts?"

"Yes! You don't know how many seem to not pick up on that," she laughed.

He didn't know why, but he felt pulled to this unknown woman and he was about to do something he never foresaw.

"Would you, ummm, would you care to dance?" Eli said, holding his hand out and bowed.

She tensed up, seeming to have an internal debate. "I would love to," she said, reaching out to take Eli's hand before pausing. "Eli?" Her gaze fell to his battered up hand.

It took only a matter of seconds to recognize the way she said his name. Even in a crowd of camouflaged people, he still found her. This would not ruin his night. "Darci?"

Darci dropped his hand and took a step back, looking him over. She would never have recognized him. His hair laid neatly in place, the suit fit so well it looked tailored to him. Maybe it was the mask, but she'd never noticed his squared jawline or the light cleft in his chin. Dare she forget how much of an ass he'd been? Darci turned to look at all the others who'd taken up partners and were dancing. Her feelings about him wouldn't overshadow the night. She wouldn't allow them to.

"Yes." She looked down at his hand. "How is your hand healing?"

"Well, actually." Eli brought his hand up and flexed his fingers, evaluating it like he hadn't just seen it moments before.

"That's good to hear." Darci looked around some more. She was embarrassed to have taken the step back, creating the distance between them. The last thing she wanted to do was give off the signal that she didn't want to dance. She bit at her red lower lip, debating on what to do next. "Look, I know we have our differences of opinion on pretty much everything," Darci fumbled out. "But would you still like to dance?"

Eli stared at her. Did she just really ask him to dance?

"Sure," Eli said, taking a step towards her, lifting his hand again.

This time Darci took it gingerly, trying to be careful of the still healing hand. The song was on its last measure by the time they made it to the dance floor, so they waited silently for the next song to start.

Eli clasped her hand in his, reaching around to place his hand on her lower back. He'd not realized until that moment, when his hand touched bare skin, her dress was backless. The charged feeling from her skin startled him.

Iris by the Goo Goo Dolls came to life in their ears. Eli stepped with his left foot, leading them in a waltz. Darci met him step by step, gliding gracefully like a swan. They made their way around the dance floor, their eyes never leaving each other.

"How did you learn to dance like this?" Darci asked, surprised.

"My grandfather and grandmother were big fans of ballroom dancing." Eli cracked a lopsided grin at the memories that flooded his mind.

"They taught you well," Darci said, a small grin of hers creeping upon her lips.

"Thank you."

"Eli, can I ask you something?"

"I suppose I'm a captive audience right now," Eli said, still grinning.

"I know you hate me. Is that the reason you won't take up the internship?"

Eli didn't have a suitable answer for that. He'd been kicking himself in the ass for the past few weeks for turning it down. His emotions seemed to get the best of him. He knew the chance had passed and made peace with it.

Darci spoke up again. "I heard from Charleigh you are looking to get into investigative journalism. I'm friends with an editor at *The Times* and can put a word in for you—if you like."

"It was just a lot. When the internship was announced, I'd not had time to evaluate things." Eli sighed. "If I'm being honest, yes. A good part of my refusal was because of you being, well, you." Darci's jaw clenched upon hearing that. "But I've had time to process it all and, if you'll still have me, I'd like to take the internship."

Bewilderment relaxed her rigid and tense posture, making her cock her head. "The internship is yours."

"Wonderful. I'll try not to let you down."

They danced the rest of the song in contemplative silence. Eli would leave all he knew behind in a matter of weeks, move to a city that held his future, and work with a woman who could make his dreams a reality. This was the start of a new chapter in both their lives.

Chapter 8

E vents from the night before played on repeat for Eli. His dance
with Darci was unexpected, and so was the outcome. The house
was quiet and he was alone chewing his half burned toast in a mild
catatonic state. There was so much to unpack, and he didn't know
where to even begin. It had been a good night. If he were being honest
with himself, one of the best in a long while. The fact that it was Darci
who made it remotely enjoyable was a tough pill to swallow. She was
the last person he'd thought he'd have fun with.

The doorbell ringing brought Eli back to the present. He shook the
thoughts from his mind, threw the dry toast on the plate in front of
him, brushed the crumbs from his hands while getting up to answer.
As far as he knew, they weren't expecting visitors so early.

Eli swung the door open, only to have the male figure push right
past him.

"Excuse me? You can't just walk into our house uninvited," Eli
stated in pure confusion and disbelief.

"Oh, dear boy. I can, this technically is my house after all," the nasally voice corrected.

He'd heard of their landlord, Mr. Collins, but had never met him. His father would change the subject if his cousin's name ever came up in conversation. There was no love between the two, it seemed. Eli couldn't imagine why after seeing his present behavior.

"Mr. Collins, I take it?"

"At your service. Where is your father?"

"Well, seeing as though you are here in the morning at an ungodly hour, my guess would be, in bed," Eli derided.

"No matter. I'll just wait until he wakes up."

Eli couldn't bring himself to do anything outside of stare and blink rapidly, trying to figure out if he was dreaming. Without looking away from the unwelcome intruder, Eli swung the door shut. There was no way he was going to remain in this room by himself, entertaining such a ridiculously rude man who was nearly twenty years older than him.

"How bout I hurry the process up for you," Eli said, bounding up the stairs to his parents' room. Eli rapped on his parents' door until he heard them stir. He refused to go back downstairs after having found a chance to escape. "You guys have a visitor," Eli yelled through the door.

His dad opened the door, rubbing the sleep from his eyes with his other hand. "A visitor? This early?" Henry groggily said.

"Yeah, and you'll really appreciate his company," Eli said sarcastically.

"Who on earth is this inconsiderate?"

"I'll give you two guesses, but think you'll only need one. Starts with a C and ends with an S."

"No." The surprise painted on his father's face was priceless.

"Yes," Eli confirmed.

"Will you please go tell him I will be down shortly?"

"Nope." Eli shook his head adamantly. "He's your cousin and I refuse to deal with him any more than I have to."

"Fine. Will you go wake up your brothers then?"

"That I will do. They can help keep Mr. Collins entertained."

Eli turned away as his father shut the door, debating on who to wake up first, though he dared not bring James into this mess. He had more respect for his brother than to do that to him. Lance and Kit, however, would be just the chaotic duo to handle Collins. Their ignorance would suit the situation well. He walked over to their door and knocked.

"Go away," Lance grumpily called out.

"No."

"Eli, I'm going to need you to take five steps back from our door, turn, and take another seven steps down the hall, turn, and take three steps forward, flinging yourself over the banister," Kit directed.

"While that would be preferable to what is downstairs waiting for us," Eli muttered under his breath. "I need your Tweedle Dum and Tweedle Dee asses to get out of bed and come downstairs," he exclaimed.

"What's downstairs?" Lance asked, curious.

"Donuts and fresh coffee." Eli smirked. He wasn't at all sorry for the lie he told.

There was a hushed mumbling in the room, unintelligible to Eli. "Okay. Give us a few minutes and we'll be down."

They were going to be pissed when they found out the truth, but that wasn't Eli's problem. He started walking to his bedroom, stopping to knock on Mark's door to make sure he was awake. After the third knock, Eli remembered what day it was, and that Mark was at church.

"Lucky bastard," Eli mumbled to himself.

He padded to James' room. Eli fully expected his brother to still be asleep when he walked in. Instead, James had already showered and was throwing on his jacket. "Where are you going?"

"Last night Charleigh invited me over for breakfast this morning and to go horseback riding after."

"That sounds fun. Too bad you can't join the rest of us in proverbial hell."

"What do you mean?"

"Mr. Collins," Eli said, holding his nose, "is downstairs right now for god knows what reason."

"Yeah. You have fun with that." James walked to the window, opening it. "Give mom and dad my apologies." He stepped through to his freedom and closed the window behind him.

"Fuck." Eli looked around the room, trying to dig up any excuse to not go back downstairs. He had nothing. He let out a defeated sigh, and resigned himself to the suffering that was in his future.

"Darci! Do I look ok?" Charleigh asked nervously.

Darci raised her eyebrows before furrowing them. "You look the same as when you asked me ten minutes ago."

"No. I put this clip in my hair! Does it look ok?"

"Char, I mean this in the nicest way possible. Why would he care about such a minor detail? He is a man. They don't care."

"That's not true. Plenty of guys care."

"Oh? Name one you've met who has cared." Darci waited a moment for Charleigh to answer before continuing. "Like I said. Wear it for you and no one else. If you like it, then wear it."

"One day, things like this will matter to you."

"I highly doubt that."

Footsteps thudded down the hallway, getting closer. Charleigh's brother strode into the room like a peacock, thinking he owned the place. He walked to the couch to sit beside Darci, propping his feet on the coffee table.

"Get your feet off the table, Karl," Darci muttered in disgust.

Karl smirked at Darci before doing as she said. "What's got you all excited, sis?"

"James is coming over in a bit for breakfast, and then I thought we would go horseback riding."

"James?" Karl looked over at Darci with a questioning face. "Do I know who this person is?"

"He is one of the Bennet brothers," Darci answered.

"You've got to be kidding me, Char." Karl's tone shifted to exasperation. "That family is a bane."

"A bane?" Charleigh's fists balled up at her side. "How so? Please. Tell me what you mean by that."

"Look, I'll not pretend that this will be okay with mom and dad."

"Mom, dad?" Charleigh threw her hands in the air. "You realize I'm an adult, right? Fully capable of making my own decisions?"

"Yes, but as an heir to the family fortune and business, they won't allow such an obvious mis-pairing." Karl glanced over at Darci. "Please help me out here?"

Darci returned the look and grabbed a magazine off the table, opening it and pretending to read an article. She was not about to interject, even if Karl was right.

"You know what, fine." Karl stood up and adjusted his pant leg. "You set yourself up for heartbreak. I wash my hands of this." Charleigh glared at Karl as he stalked out of the room.

Darci didn't look up from the magazine. "You know he is right."

"Not you too, Darci," Charleigh chided.

Darci closed the magazine, tossed it on the table and crossed her arms in front of her chest. "The reasoning is valid and you need to really ask yourself, is this worth setting yourself up for disappointment and heartbreak?"

Sounds of gravel being crushed filled the silence, as Darci and Charleigh stared one another down, both standing their ground. Charleigh broke her stare first, walking to the window to confirm it was James.

"I don't have time for this," Charleigh huffed. She moved to the coat rack, grabbing the tool needed to make her great escape. To hammer home her ire and give her a small semblance of control, Charleigh slammed the door behind her.

"Are you all right?" James asked.

"James, would you be too upset if we did the horse back riding first and ate breakfast after? I need to clear my head and be away from here for a bit."

"Sure. I have to warn you, I've never ridden a horse before." James gazed down at his scuffed up and worn tennis shoes.

"Oh, it's easy. I'll help you. Follow me."

Charleigh took off around the back of the house, not giving James the chance to keep up. James took in his surroundings for a moment. Ashen clouds swirled about the sky in contrast to the pearly white, towering abode in front of him. The realization of how out of place he was felt like a boulder weighing him down. His legs wouldn't move him from that spot. There were forces at work and they would have to be divine in their efforts if Charleigh and he were ever to be together. It was unfair that one's circumstances of their birth and family connections should dictate one's life. That she was born to a wealthy family and he a family of meager means was all happenstance. Nothing that either of them could control; not their upbringing, nor who their hearts loved.

"James?" Charleigh called out, peeking around the corner of the house.

"Coming." James strode up the path to catch up.

They moved in step towards the stable hand, who held the reins of two thoroughbred horses. One was chestnut colored, with a thick white band traveling from its forehead down to its muzzle. The other a marbled gray. These formidable muscular beasts exuded majesty. Their bobbing heads enchanted James, beckoning him to them.

"They are beautiful, Charleigh. What are their names?"

Charleigh walked to the reddish brown one, petting his mane. "This is Tristan. That," she nodded her head towards the other horse, "is Isolde."

James moved to the side of Isolde and ran his fingers down her forehead, moving to her cheek while looking at Charleigh. "Beautiful."

Charleigh ducked her head, the heat welling up shading her face in a light pink hue, and smiled. "I think you should ride Isolde. She's much more tame for those new to riding." James nodded his head, moving to the side, taking the reins in his hand.

"Have you ever mounted a horse before?" The stable hand inquired.

James chuckled nervously. "I haven't."

"Names Jacob. Alright, would you like me to explain?"

"I'd appreciate that, Jacob." James took a step back, allowing the groomer to check the saddle and stirrups.

"Okay. Grab the horn and back of the saddle. Put your left foot in the stirrup using it as leverage to throw your other leg over."

James gave a slight nod. He placed his hands where the gentleman said to, stuck his left foot in the stirrup, and attempted to swing his leg up, hitting the saddle with his right leg, falling. Jacob caught him before he hit the ground.

"Thanks," James huffed, startled.

"You're welcome. It's always difficult when doing this for the first time. Let me help brace you."

James began again, allowing Jacob to help push his right leg over. He slid his foot into the other stirrup and adjusted his weight on the saddle. "How do I get her to move?"

Charleigh let out a giggle. "Squeeze the horse's ribcage with your calves." James nodded, looking down at his legs while he squeezed. Isolde whinnied in response and clopped forward a bit. "Now, to direct her, you want to use the reins." Charleigh mounted Tristan and clicked her tongue on her cheek, moving herself next to James. " You hold them like this." She reached over, brushing against the skin on his hand and froze. Her face tilted up to gaze into his eyes, willing him to lean in and kiss her.

James' lips parted. He knew she wanted more of him in that moment than he would give in the company of Jacob. No, she'd have to wait until they were far into the woods. Once he started, it would be hell to stop. He had dreamed of the feeling of his lips moving up her neck slowly, placing tiny kisses along her vein. The feeling of her body, wrapped in his, shuttering as he lightly traced over her curves. He needed to stop his brain from going any further down the dream rabbit hole. He broke their stare and readjusted himself in the saddle.

"I think I've watched enough westerns to figure out that the direction you tug the reins on dictates the direction of the horse," he grunted out, still battling his desires.

Charleigh's eyes fell to his hands. "Yes. And when you want to stop, pull the reins back." She looked up at James, who was busy running through the motions of steering Isolde. Her heart sank knowing the moment had passed, and he'd done nothing with it. Maybe he didn't want her that way after all.

Chapter 9

Charleigh clicked her tongue again and gave Tristan a squeeze around his midsection, prodding him to move at a steady pace forward. James followed suit, aiming to settle in beside Charleigh. They rode in silence for several minutes. Both waiting for the other to make the first move after the charged moment between them. James kept glancing behind them, watching the house get smaller in the distance. He couldn't wait to have the freedom to show Charleigh his true feelings. They'd not had a minute alone without someone's watchful eye, and it annoyed him and he didn't know when he would get another opportunity.

With one last glance to make sure the house was nowhere in sight, James pulled back on the reins, bringing Isolde to a halt. Charleigh followed suit and twisted around to stare back at James.

"Are you okay? I know you've been looking back at the house a lot," Charleigh sighed. "James, do you want to leave? I can take it if you just don't want to do this—" she gestured between them with her free hand, "anymore." Her jaw clenched as she tried to restrain the tears that gathered in her eyes.

James felt the sting of the arrow she hurled at his heart. He didn't know if the brush off was intentionally nonchalant as to hide her genuine emotions or if she truly was that indifferent. All he knew is he had to find out which it was and there was only one way to do that. He leaned to the side, throwing his leg over, and slid down the side of Isolde. He gripped the reins as he walked up beside Tristan. His hand ran over Charleigh's jeans, the rough fabric catching on the tiny calluses on his palms. He hoped she didn't mind a worker's hands. Her leg tensed at his touch.

"I'd very much like to stay here with you," James said. His hand reached her hip, and he gave it a squeeze. It was the only way he could think to communicate his needs to her.

Charleigh peered down at him. Her breath came out ragged. She nodded, throwing her leg over Tristan and slid the full of her body against him. James' breath hitched, feeling the weight of her pressed against him. All he focused on was the flame in her eyes. She felt the same as he did. He was sure of it.

"I'm want to kiss you." His breath, hot and sticky in the crisp air, was the essence of what they both were feeling.

Charleigh stood on her toes, taking his face in her hands, and moved her mouth closer to his. "Please, do."

That was all he needed. Reins fell from his hand; the world melted away. He bent down, allowing her better access to run her fingers through his hair, and pressed his lips against hers. His freed hand rose and caressed her neck, pulling her closer. A hunger welled up in him, one he'd never felt before, and it scared him. There'd be no going back. He needed to be sure she understood that and agreed.

James broke the kiss, lightly tracing his thumb over her cheek to her lips. He outlined where his mouth had just been, tasting her for the first time. "Charleigh, I've wanted to do that for so long," his voice a low raspy whisper. His other hand ran down her back, stopping to cup her backside. "There is more I would like to do if you'll allow it." He bent down and traced her neck with his lips, sending a shiver up her spine.

"Oh, James." Charleigh nuzzled into his shoulder, allowing him better access to her. "I want you."

James nibbled on her earlobe, whispering, "Good," through the tiny bites. He broke away and walked back towards Isolde which left Charleigh whimpering for more of him. "Do you think we can ride to the corner store just down the way?"

Charleigh shook her head, still struggling to get her wits about her. "We don't have to." She reached back out, inviting James to take his place again. "It's okay," Charleigh said with a reassuring smile.

James nodded in understanding and turned back to his haven. He stormed over, picked her up and carried her further into the woods off the path. Her arms around him felt good. There was something primal about carrying her. She ran one hand up and down his chest, working the buttons on his shirt that lay exposed from the open jacket, while the other clutched his neck.

He sucked in a deep breath as the chilled air hit his bare chest. This was the most ludicrous thing he had ever done, but she was the only person he wanted to share this moment with. Her finger tips swirled in random patterns as she took in his heat, making it her own. He couldn't wait any longer. His mouth came down hard on her as he lowered her to the ground on top a leaf pile. The realization smacked him as he sat back on his heels, gazing into the eyes of the goddess before him, taking in her beauty.

"James?" Charleigh sat up on her elbows. "Is everything alright?"

"Char—" James crawled over, laying on his side next to her. "I never want to spend a moment of my life without you in it." Charleigh laid back down, turning to face him, propping her head on her bent arm.

James trailed his fingertips down the side of her ribs and settled just above her hip, pausing before moving his hand under the top of her jeans. Charleigh laid back on the ground, moving to the button on her jeans. "No." James grabbed her hands, gently placing them on her belly. "I want to enjoy this."

Charleigh nodded, her hands finding his face. She ran them lovingly over every inch she could see and touch. James came down on her lips again, prying with his tongue for deeper access. He desperately needed more, and she willingly gave it. He worked the button to her jeans, and with a twist, undid it. His hand crept further down, forcing the zipper to abide by his will. The satin of her panties awoke the desire to feel more of her. He slid his fingers between the barrier, keeping him from the warmth between her legs. Charleigh threw her head back, arching toward his hand as he gently stroked her. She sucked in a breath as he focused on where she needed his finger the most. He watched her face as he went back for more, waiting to see how her body responded to him. Her body arched again and her mouth hung open as she inhaled deeply, eyes closed.

"James," her hands moved to his back, clutching his jacket, to ground herself to get the words out. "I need you." He flicked over again, forcing her to pause. "I need to feel you. Please."

James held his free hand under her head, lifting her to him. As their mouths met, longing poured out of them both. He slid his hand down, thrusting two fingers inside of her. Charleigh grabbed at his back, moaning in pleasure. He worked rhythmically, building up her release, wanting to feel her soft and wet tightening.

He relished how she moved her hips in time, begging for more. Her moans were music to his ears. She was riding her own wave of ecstasy now. Her arms braced themselves around him, as the surge hit, and she gave way to the ripples of rapture. Charleigh relaxed her arms, falling back to look at James. "I love you," she pushed out through gasps of air.

James' heartbeat raced at the admission. Blood pounded in his ears. He'd been fighting himself, attempting to keep the lions at bay, so he wouldn't accidentally say those three words before she was ready. Since the moment he saw her, he knew there was something about her, and having spent every waking day with her these last few months affirmed that. Lions be damned. He'd give them what they craved. James looked down at the woman laying before him, her cheeks flushed. "I love you, too."

At his words, Charleigh rose, pushing James to sit up. She straddled her legs on either side of his thighs and began trailing kisses down the side of his neck, moving her hands to let his jacket and shirt fall off. Her finger tips trailed down his back. Nails dug in as she rocked, feeling his want for her between her legs.

"Let's make this even," Charleigh said with a wide grin. She grabbed her shirt, pulled it over her head, discarding it.

James placed his hands on her hips and nuzzled into her neck and chest, running his lips over her exposed skin. He could better smell the vibrant orange and hints of may rose body wash she liked to bathe with. Everything about her was elegant. He rued the day when she would wake up and see him for what he was, but until that day, he would enjoy living in the moment with her.

"Hey, where did you go?" Charleigh asked.

"I'm sorry. I just—You're perfect," James said, devouring her with his eyes.

Charleigh bent her head. Redness crept up from her neck to her beautifully angled face. James took a hand off her hips, cupping her chin, forcing her to look at him. He gazed into her eyes, hoping that all he felt poured out of him into her. "I—I," Charleigh tried to find the words. She'd just have to show him.

Her lips pressed to his again, claiming him as hers. His hands left their position and wrapped around her, pulling her warmth to him. The feeling of her skin on his made the tiny hairs on the back of his neck stand straight on end. Her nipples grazed his chest as she moved up and down. He knew he couldn't hold back much longer. The need to feel her around him overcame him.

James moved forward, laying her back on the ground. His hands busied themselves, working to pull off her riding boots one at a time. It was impossibly hard to concentrate with Charleigh taking it upon herself to stroke him through his jeans, while gingerly working to free him. He placed her boots out of the way and grabbed her pants from the waist and moved them down, taking in every inch of her. As they slid past her hips, he saw the product of her arousal. He discarded her pants on top of her boots and paused, taking in the artwork that lay before him and committing to memory every detail of this moment.

Charleigh watched as he took her in. James let out a groan and pulled off his jeans and boxers, tossing them over to where her clothes laid. He was no longer in charge. This was what they both wanted, no, needed. He lowered himself down, pulling her panties off before settling in between her legs. Her eyes, his sole focus. He wanted to see every flicker of emotion and live every moment of this with her. With one arm bracing himself up, he used his hand to guide himself inside of her.

Charleigh gasped. "God, James," she said, digging her nails into his back.

As his name escaped her lips, he sank deep inside of her, causing her to arch towards him. She wrapped her legs around him, signaling, like a horse, what she wanted. James grinned to himself. She was easy to read if you knew how to pay attention to her cues. He continued to thrust, each time building up more power behind it. Her legs guided him. If she wanted him to linger deep inside of her, she would dig her heels into his buttocks and hold him there. Should she prefer he move about freely, she released her grip on his ass. Or, if she wanted him to thrust in and out faster, she would push her heels in and let go repeatedly, building up to the tempo in step with his moving inside of her.

James took it all in, memorizing every curve of her body, while they shared in their release together.

Chapter 10

E li's brain was numb. He'd sat there in the same place on the couch for hours. Everyone was to remain in place and entertain their guest. Lance and Kit sat across from him, pretending to pay attention, though it was clear they had zoned out. Mark had his nose in some religious self-help book. Mr. Collins was an insufferable man, one that Eli couldn't ever see attracting a mate. That he droned on like Ben Stein in *Ferris Bueller's Day Off* was enough to render anyone unfortunate enough to draw his attention brain dead.

They'd all discussed the events of the party, family matters, and it now landed squarely on business. Eli threw his head back. The dull throbbing ache was only getting worse as time dragged on.

"Now, Henry," Mr. Collins stated. "You're now climbing in your years, yet you've not solidified a plan for what'll happen in the event of your death, more specifically, what you'd like to happen with this property."

"Mr. Collins! I'd prefer you to not discuss such things about my husband," Jane said while fanning her face with her hands.

Eli saw where this was headed. His mother always flushed and attempted to self soothe with hand flaps before she reached global meltdown temperatures. Honestly, the fact it hadn't happened sooner surprised him.

"It's alright, Jane." Henry patted her hand. "It's a conversation that needs to be had, though I don't think it wise in the present company," he said, eyeing their kids.

It always came as a shock to Eli when his father humored his mother. They'd been married for decades, and he wasn't sure if the love was still there, but knew they held deep mutual respect for each other. Their marriage helped guide Eli's stance on relationships all together. He'd be damned if he wound up like his parents. If, and this was a big if, he fell in love, it would be deep and passionate.

"Very well, Henry. I'll retire to the room for a spell." Jane rose, nodded to Mr. Collins and went up the stairs.

"I'm going to be frank with you, William. I don't pretend to understand or grasp why on a Sunday morning you felt it necessary to wake our entire household up for this." Henry leaned forward, placing his arms on his knees, clasping his hands together. "But it makes no difference to me if you have a plan now or in your hand after I've keeled over. No. You made the trip here because you want me to tell you that you're officially set to inherit everything your father willed to me."

"Excuse me, we're family, and it is only out of sheer concern that I even made the trip here. Clearly, you've misjudged my intentions. My father writing in his will that you and your family were to live in this house doesn't mean you own the property. Naturally, I wouldn't seek to remove your family upon your death," William said, a scathing reprimand. Henry locked eyes with William. "I thought it would behoove me to help you settle affairs while I was in town."

Eli lifted his head off the back of the couch and peered over at the two men. "Clearly," he mumbled under his breath, smirking.

"Do you have something to say, boy?" William spat out.

Eli glared back at Mr. Collins, fighting the urge to unleash ungodly amounts of snark in his direction. It was a futile battle. Kit and Lance saw Eli's fists ball up, looked at each other, nodded in agreement, and ran back to their room. "Yes," Eli stated, while standing up from the couch. "I have something to say."

Mr. Collins stood, meeting Eli face to face. "I'm waiting."

"I suspect that you've no one in your life that cares that you exist." Eli rubbed his chin before carrying on. "It's the only reason I can see why you'd be here injecting yourself where you're not wanted," Eli crossed his arms, "Regarding the matter at hand. You'll be lucky if you get a notice for the funeral."

"Are you going to let your son talk to me like this, Henry?" William looked back at Eli's father, waiting for him to rise in defense of his slighted cousin.

Henry sighed and stood up. "I'll not silence him from speaking his mind." Mr. Bennet moved to place himself between Eli and William. "I actually encourage free thinking in this house."

William scoffed in disgust. "It would do you well to teach your son some manners and about respecting elders."

"I don't have a problem respecting elders, or anyone if they are worth respecting. You're just a pain in the ass that we have to put up with because of DNA," Eli admonished.

The ring of the phone was divine intervention, seeing as though his big mouth was hellbent on starting a fight. Eli turned away from the raging inferno that stood before him and walked to the kitchen. The corded phone glided off the receiver while fireworks shooting off in the living room made it hard to hear the caller's words.

Eli placed a finger in his ear, hoping to hear more clearly. "Hello?"

"James!" Charleigh's voice was frantic. "Oh god—Eli?"

"Charleigh?"

"Eli! You need to get here now." Charleigh sobbed.

"What's happened?"

"James had an accident. Oh god—"

"Charleigh! Where are you?" Eli yelled.

"Oh, Eli. I'm so sorry."

"Where are you?" Eli demanded.

"We're here at Netherfield."

"I'll be right there," Eli said, slamming the phone back on the hook.

He rushed from the kitchen back to the living room where it had grown silent thanks to them hearing his end of the conversation.

"Who was that, Eli? What happened?" Henry asked.

"That was Charleigh. Something happened to James. I'm going over there now."

Henry nodded and looked at William. "This will have to wait until another day. Let me show you out."

Eli ran past his father and Mr. Collins, skipping stairs as he sprinted up to his room, rushing to put on his shoes. He'd been trying to think of a reason to escape the house for hours. This was not a reason he cared for.

Tightness in his chest reminded Eli that it'd been too long since he ran like this. His time on the Meryton High track team seemed a distant memory. He used to run 5 miles easily, often clocking in around twenty-five minutes. Now he was pushing 40 minutes. Gravel ground beneath his feet as he rounded the corner, entering through the wrought-iron gate that hung open. Eli slowed his pace, the urgent feeling dissipating. He raised his hands above his head, taking deep breaths to calm the violent thudding in his chest and level out his breathing. Sweat trickled down the side of his face, dripping off the tip of his nose and chin.

Eli climbed the stairs to the house, walking straight into the unlocked home. Let them yell at him for not waiting for an invitation to enter. He had more important things to be concerned with. "Charleigh?" Eli yelled out while he began walking from the foyer down the hallway. "Charleigh?"

The layout of the rooms in the house, outside the main ones he'd been in at the party, was unfamiliar to him. Eli sighed in response to the silence and resigned himself to open every door he came across. The first door was a simple coat closet. His feet sloshed in the pools of rainwater his sneakers collected, squeaking on the waxed floor as he walked to the second door, twisting the handle and pulling it open. Eli poked his head in the room and immediately regretted doing so.

"Eli?"

He knew that voice. His back straightened and sat in the doorway trying to think how to deal with this.

"Eli?" an unfamiliar voice parroted.

It was too late. Eli stepped over the threshold into the library, giving the inhabitants a full view of his unkempt state. The sound of water escaping his shoes and mud falling off the soles announced his every step. His gray sweatpants felt the weight of the muddy field he'd run through while the dingy white t-shirt he wore stuck to his chest and back, glued in place by perspiration.

"Dear god." The unfamiliar man grimaced, revolted by Eli's sloven appearance.

Eli eyed the oblong face, studying his features. Icy blue-gray, deep-set eyes framed with manicured straight eyebrows bore into him. His firm, thin lips were accentuated with a narrow, straight, and thin mustache. By far, the most prominent feature was the man's high-bridged nose that also sported a defined curve midway down. Muscles of the angular jaw with a protruding dimpled chin flexed as he clenched his jaw. His ash-blonde hair was styled in a slicked back, side part. "I'm looking for James." Eli's eyes locked onto Darci. He didn't have time to worry about what this person thought. It was of no consequence to him.

Darci nodded, getting up from the desk, brushing past the repulsed person. "Follow me."

"Hopefully, you plan to take him out to the stables where he belongs."

Darci rolled her eyes in response as they walked through the doorway. She turned back, staring daggers at the individual before retorting. "If only more people saw the benefits of exercise, maybe there would be less miserable sods in the world." Darci closed the door behind her. "Karl can be a chore."

"Are you and Karl–together?" The pangs of jealousy stabbed at him, though he didn't understand why. What did he care if she was in a relationship?

Laughter escaped from Darci. "Charleigh's brother. Though I suspect they both would like that to be the case."

They stopped for a moment at the base of the stairs, their eyes meeting. Eli felt warmth swell up in the pit of his stomach. The hell was wrong with him? Both seemed dumbfounded by the pause, breaking their gaze at the same time. Eli ran his fingers through his drenched hair.

Darci cleared her throat. "If you go up the stairs, three doors down to your right, you'll find the guest bedroom James is in. Charleigh is with him."

When Eli entered the room, he found Charleigh standing at the end of the bed. He followed her gaze down to his brother, laying propped up with pillows. She looked over towards Eli, her brow furrowed with worry. "I called my doctor. I didn't know what to do."

"Eli, can you please tell Charleigh I'm fine," James asked.

Eli walked over to her, placed his hand on her shoulder. "What happened?"

Charleigh ran her shirt sleeve along her red nose, and James crossed his arms across his chest. "We went horseback riding," James said.

"I just don't know what set her off," Charleigh said.

"Set who off?" Eli asked.

"Isolde," Charleigh and James said in unison.

"She's not easily spooked," Charleigh added and looked back at James. "I should have warned you to not move too fast behind them," she said. Charleigh glanced at Eli. "He didn't know."

"You're not responsible for any of this. It was just an accident, Charleigh," Eli said. "Did the horse kick you, James?"

A small chuckle left James. "You'd think so, going off Charleigh's hysterics."

Charleigh shot James a sharp look and sniffed a few times. "That would have been so much worse." She hung her head, dejected. "I got his attention before her hoof hit him. He dove missing the kick but hit his head on the ground."

"Charleigh, I've been hurt worse fighting with Eli," James said.

"So you've said several times," Charleigh quipped. "I called my doctor to make a house call anyway, just in case," she said, shrugging.

"What did the doctor say," Eli asked.

"That what happened could have been bad, but because James landed like he did, it's nothing more than a mild concussion." She looked back at James.

"He said I'll be fine, but that I need to rest for the next day or two," James looked over at Charleigh, "which I can do at home."

Charleigh shook her head and rolled her eyes. "Will you please talk James into staying tonight, Eli? He's being stubborn and I just want to make sure he is okay."

Her concern for James was sweet, even if it was a tad overdone. He could see the pleading in her eyes. Eli nodded. If James staying the night would make her feel more comfortable, surely James could humor her. "James, I'm inclined to agree with Charleigh. I think you'd get more rest here than at *home*."

James looked between Eli and Charleigh and nodded. "You're probably right, Eli."

"Can I use the phone to call my parents to tell them what's going on, Charleigh," Eli asked.

"Sure! There is one in my bedroom across the hall."

"Thanks." Eli walked to the door before looking back once more. There was so much love between the two, anyone who couldn't see it was a fool.

Chapter 11

Scalding hot water poured from the shower head when he turned on the faucet, a pleasant surprise and something he wasn't used to. Eli stepped into the stone standalone, focusing the powerful stream on the tension he'd carried between his shoulder blades, melting it away.

Charleigh wanted him to stay, and he'd agreed against his better judgment. She looked so upset and it was the right thing to do. James would have done the same if it were him in that bed. He only needed to manage dinner and departing. He could do this.

Eli sighed, resigning himself to the task at hand, turned the water off, and stepped out of the shower. The air hit his wet body, chilling him. He wrapped the towel around his waist and moved to the fogged up mirror, using his hand to wipe it clean. The reflection that stared back at him spoke silent truths he'd attempted to push down. Things had gotten complicated quickly. He felt trapped. His mind was stuck spinning uncontrollably and he couldn't figure out how to get off the rollercoaster.

Nothing had been simple since the Netherfield party. James had found Charleigh, and he'd done nothing but dote on her since. Even Chase had little time for him. It was a lonely existence being locked in one's head.

The towel fell from his waist as he wiped up the dripping streams of water from his chest. Eli looked over at the set of clothes on the bathroom counter. Charleigh meant well providing a change of clothes from her brother's wardrobe, but they were another box Eli had to force himself into, pretending he was someone he wasn't. He played the part of imposter well as he'd felt like one many times in his life, more so lately.

He grabbed the silk button up long-sleeve shirt and peeked at the tag. "Versace." Great, a shirt that not only made him uncomfortable because of its style, but now he had to worry about ruining it. It must've cost a fortune. His arms slid into the holes effortlessly, the silk sticking to the moisture on his back in the most uncomfortable way. If the shirt felt like this, he couldn't wait for the pants.

Eli rubbed the material of the pants, not able to place the fabric. He lifted them, debating on if he should even look at the tag. Curiosity got the best of him, as it did most times. "Givenchy, Italian virgin wool," Eli mumbled. *What does virgin wool even mean?* Eli shook the thought from his head. He didn't care what it meant.

He pushed his legs through the leg holes and pulled them up, letting the waist settle on his hips. The fit wasn't too far off from his size, though a little short in the legs. They would have to do. Eli set to fastening the pants when there was a knock on the door. Without thinking, Eli pulled it open, meeting widened eyes and a gaping mouth.

"I, uh, dinner, umm, is hot," Darci stammered out breathlessly. "I'm ready-" her face flushed as she stumbled over her words. "I mean, dinner is ready." She turned away, grumbling to herself as she walked down the hallway, her hands moving through the air as she was talking.

Eli peeked around the doorjamb and watched in fascination until she turned the corner, leaving him in a weirdly pleased state. He ran his fingers through his hair and shut the door, leaning against it. His hands ran down the shirt, fingers working the buttons, while Darci's stumbled words replayed.

Aromas of warm spices and savory meat filled the air as Eli walked past the kitchen. He backtracked, sticking his head in through the open door. A woman dressed in black stood in front of a pot on the stove, stirring. Plates and bowls lined the counter tops, waiting to be filled.

"Excuse me," Eli said, stepping just inside the doorway.

The woman jumped and turned to face him. "Oh, you scared me. Sorry, I was staring off into space."

"I didn't mean to scare you, my apologies."

"No worries. What can I help you with?" Her voice was soft and kind.

"I don't know my way around this place and am trying to find where everyone is," Eli said. "I looked in the dining room, but no one was there."

"Ah. Yes, they decided they'd eat in the sunroom because of the open atmosphere."

"Oh, okay," Eli moved his body to the doorway, pointing his hands in conflicting directions. "Which way is that?"

"To your left and through the door you'll see off the living room. I'm about to serve the first course."

"Thank you—" Eli waited for her to fill in her name.

"Sheila."

Eli grinned. "Oh, and would you mind sending dinner to my brother?"

Sheila smiled. "Ms. Bingley has already instructed me to do so."

Eli nodded. "Thank you, Sheila."

He found the living room easily and spotted a sliding glass door hidden in the corner. Eli walked over, pausing before sliding the door open. The flicker of candlelight danced about, casting silhouettes of the floral centerpieces on the dark wooden table. Chairs with decorative scroll cutouts lined the sides. Towards one end sat Charleigh, her laughter making her eyes small. Darci sat next to her, staring straight ahead at the face of the dark blonde who sat in front of her. He studied her face, trying to see if she had laughed too, and surmised she'd been lost in her own thoughts, given the blank stare that seemed to peer through the guy. He slid the door open with ease, alerting his hosts of his arrival.

"Oh good," Charleigh exclaimed. "You found us."

"I did, with the help of Sheila."

"Wonderful. She is the best chef in the county."

Karl turned to face Eli, looking him up and down. "If I hadn't seen the wildness earlier, I'd say you were a proper gentleman." Karl turned back around and looked at Darci. "If only clothes could fix the station of one in society."

Karl's words broke the trance Darci had been in. The table scraped the tiled floor as it moved under the force that Eli could surmise was an under the table kick, looking at Karl's body shudder. Though he couldn't tell who administered the righteous punishment.

"Karl scoot down so Eli can sit by me," Charleigh commanded.

"I don't want to cause an issue, Charleigh."

"Nonsense, Eli. He can move. After all, you're our guest."
Charleigh's joyful personality had eased back into place. Eli was envious of how easy it seemed, like flipping a switch on. He could see why James was taken with her. Eli took the seat that Karl had evacuated. Instead of moving a seat down, Karl had gone around the table and sat next to Darci. He could feel the cold that radiated from Karl through the overpriced garb. "So, Eli, how was the shower? The clothes seem to fit okay."

"It was—" Eli looked over at Darci, who was sipping her glass of wine, a smirk crawling across his face. "Hot and ready—rather quickly."

Darci grabbed the napkin from her lap and pressed it to her mouth to suppress the coughing fit that ensued. Karl raised her other arm and pounded on her back. Her throat cleared several times before she looked at Eli, shooting daggers at him.

"Are you okay?" Eli asked nonchalantly.

Darci's voice, still croaky from the coughing, met him in tone. "Never better."

They stared at each other for a moment until Sheila slid the door open, pushing in a serving cart. She went around the table, placing the bowls of lobster bisque in front of each person, before going back to the cart, grabbing two baskets of fresh garlic knots, and setting them on the table.

Eli had never seen such a sight, nor partaken in anything so refined. He looked down at the assortment of utensils at his disposal. Why did a person need more than one fork? The spoon above his plate looked too small to be for soup, so he opted for the one to the right of the one of two knives. He looked around to study those around him to see if he had guessed right. It was a win.

Charleigh grabbed a garlic knot from the basket and put it on the small plate to the left of her small spoon and fork above the plate and used the other knife laid across the tiny plate to cut the bread. Eli took a silverware count and deduced that the person who was to wash all these dishes must hate their life. All of it was so needless and over done. He'd never been much of a wine drinker, but tonight would see that he drank it with no qualms. He only hoped there would be enough to get him through the evening.

"So, Mr. Bennet—" Karl started.

"Just Eli. Mr. Bennet is my dad."

"Okay then, Eli, what is your occupation?"

He knew as soon as the words left Karl's mouth that any response he gave wouldn't be good enough. Karl seemed to have it out for him, and he didn't understand why. Eli had never interacted with the man. The only reason Eli could think of for Karl's disdain was the fact his family was poor. "Well, I attend Meryton University as a full-time student, but sell articles as a freelance writer to the Meryton Press ."

"Ah, so you don't hold a full-time job then? Pardon my asking, how can you afford your own place without working?"

"I still live with my parents. We decided when I got the full ride scholarship to save money where we could regarding paying for the dorms."

"And what of your brother?"

"Which one." Eli deadpanned.

"You have more than the one?"

"Yes, I have four in total."

"Ah, I suppose your parents didn't figure out until it was too late how not making babies works."

"Excuse me?"

Darci and Charleigh watched the interactions like a Wimbledon tennis match until that point. "Your brothers are lovely, Eli. I only wish my parents would have blessed me with having more siblings." Charleigh peered at Karl. "Maybe then I wouldn't be stuck in the company of this jerk as much as I have been." Karl glared back at Charleigh and ate the rest of his soup in silence. "Darci tells me you got placement as an intern at De Bourgh Publishing?"

"Yes, an incredible opportunity." Eli looked from Karl to Darci and then to Charleigh. "It was a surprise award, as the class didn't know about it."

"It certainly helps when you have a cousin who is a bigwig," Charleigh laughed.

"How do you like Professor Fitzwilliam?" Darci chimed in.

Eli looked across the table at Darci. The candle light made her eyes glitter. He didn't know if this was a ploy to get him to put his foot in his mouth as he had so many times before, but he would avoid that pitfall. "I find him an effective teacher. He has the perfect balance of humor and conciseness that I appreciate." Eli drank the rest of the wine from his glass and held it in his hand, staring through the glass at his hand. "I believe that a great teacher is a great artist and that teaching might be the greatest of the arts, since the medium is the human mind and spirit."

"Steinbeck."

"Yes." Eli looked from the glass to Darci, setting the glass down in front of him.

"The mind is not a vessel to be filled, but a fire to be kindled." Darci said softly.

"Plutarch."

"Yes."

Charleigh's mouth fell open slightly before she rapidly closed it. "So, umm, Eli. How is James doing?" Charleigh squeaked out.

Eli's attention turned from Darci to Charleigh. "Oh, he's fine. Annoyed at me for insisting he stay in bed, but he chilled out when I told him we'd leave tomorrow morning."

"Oh?" Charleigh's voice fell in disappointment.

"I think he'll rest better at home, in his bed, with all his things," Eli said, trying to cheer Charleigh up. "You've done so much for him and our family. We won't forget it." Eli smiled.

They spent the rest of the dinner with Charleigh, telling wild stories of Darci and Karl growing up. Most of them featured Charleigh and Karl as the ones with the inane ideas and Darci working tirelessly to clean up their mess or talk them down. It certainly explained the stick in the mud persona Darci had settled into.

Chapter 12

The night wasn't kind to Eli. It was hard sleeping in an unfamiliar place and he felt more tired waking than he did turning in for the night. He'd be happy to leave and not look back after the events of last night. Charleigh did her best to soothe tensions between Karl and him, though it was in vain. Karl clearly thought ill of him as Eli did of Karl. Eli pushed the covers off him, getting up and stretching the stiffness that had settled into his bones. He had to have slept in weird positions while also tossing and turning.

A gentle knock sounded. "Eli? Are you awake?"

At the sound of Charleigh's voice, Eli walked over to the door and pulled it open. Charleigh stood before him, his clothes folded and in her hands. "Good morning, Charleigh." Eli leaned against the doorjamb, letting the door swing open wider.

"I know you mentioned wanting to take James home this morning, so I asked the maid to wash your clothes for you." Charleigh handed Eli the clean, perfectly folded squares. "I also called my doctor in to do a final check-up."

"You didn't need to call him Charleigh."

"Oh, it's alright. I just wanted to be sure James was okay to travel back home."

"Charleigh, you act like we live hours away." Eli couldn't hold back the small chuckle. It was sweet the way she was fawning over his brother.

"I know it's silly. Darci said the same thing, but I just wanted to have him checked one more time for my peace of mind."

"Fair. Thank you for having my clothes washed," Eli said, grinning.

"You're welcome." Charleigh turned to walk away before coming back to where Eli stood. "Will you miss any classes today?"

"Yeah, but I already wrote the day off. I know my professors will understand."

Charleigh nodded again, turned and strode down the hallway, making her way downstairs. Eli shut the door. It'd be good to feel comfortable again and like himself. After dressing, he tried to remake the bed in the fashion it'd been in when he arrived, though he couldn't remember the order of the overly decorated pillows that served no purpose other than to be annoying. He never understood the allure of having so many pillows you couldn't use on a bed. Waste of space and resources as far as he was concerned.

Once satisfied with the haphazardly strewn about fluff bags, he opened the door and made his way into James' room. The doctor was talking to James, who sat wide awake in the bed. Eli circled round to the other side of the bed and waited patiently while the doctor gave James directions and a verbal list of signs and symptoms to watch out for before releasing him.

"Are you related to the patient?" the doctor inquired.

"His brother."

"I need to get your John Hancock on a few forms before he can go."

"Okay." The doctor handed Eli a few pages of documentation and he glanced through them to make sure it was all standard care and procedure before signing. He gave the papers back to the doctor and looked at James. "Ready to get the hell out of here?"

James grinned at his brother. "Absolutely."

It took them a bit to get James dressed. A couple light-headed spells worked diligently against Eli's effort to get James out of there. They made their way down the hallway and came to a stop at the landing. Karl, Darci, and Charleigh stood by the door, waiting to bid farewell.

"James!" Charleigh bounded up to James and threw her arm around him. The grip Eli had on James' arm faltered. Eli pushed against Charleigh's thrusted weight, fighting to keep James upright. James wobbled but steadied himself, using his free arm to wrap around Charleigh's waist, anchoring him.

"Hey Char," James cooed in her ear. "Thank you for taking such good care of me." He placed a kiss on her cheek.

"Thank you for everything you've all done," James said, looking at Darci and Karl.

"Glad you're feeling better," Karl gave James a curt nod towards the door.

James let go of Charleigh. They walked down the remaining steps, going at James' pace. Eli helped James into the front seat of the van before shutting the door and climbing into the driver's seat. As they pulled away from Netherfield, James stared out the window, his eyes never leaving Charleigh. "I'm going to marry her."

Tuesday morning came too soon. Eli had struggled to get to sleep, which was odd given how tired he was falling into his own bed. He'd hit the snooze button so many times on his alarm it had taken Lance banging on his door to wake him up. If he hurried, he might make it to class on time.

He rushed around throwing clothes on, forgoing the shower, and grabbed a package of Pop-Tarts from the cabinet in the kitchen before running out the door. It wasn't his first choice in breakfasts but he'd little time for much else. The bus ride to the campus seemed to take longer than normal, but Eli chalked it up to the urgency welling up in his stomach. He'd prided himself on his punctuality and being behind schedule put him on edge. Doors to the auditorium were already closed when he arrived. He hoped to sneak in unnoticed, but the squeaky hinges betrayed him.

"Ah, good to see you could join us, Mr. Bennet," Professor Fitzwilliam said. Eli hung his head as he speedily made for his seat next to Chase. "As I was saying," Professor Fitzwilliam pushed his glasses further up the bridge of his nose, "I have worked very hard to put together this panel of literary agents and publishers for you. We will discuss the publishing process and will allow for questions at the end." The professor carried on naming each panelist, sharing their education and profession.

"What happened?" Chase whispered under his breath.

"I didn't sleep well last night and missed my alarm, multiple times," Eli said quietly, not looking away from the stage.

"Busy weekend then?"

"You could say that. I'll fill you in after class."

The first panelist introduced herself. "Good morning. I'm Gianna Wickham. Literary agent and working to build my publishing company as I speak."

Eli's attention went to the speaker and then to the far end of the stage where Darci sat, arms crossed with discontent painted all over her face. He couldn't fathom what perturbed her. It wasn't until Gianna began talking about her experiences in the publishing world that Darci apparently had had enough, exiting through the side door.

Gianna's attention flew to the closing door briefly before she refocused on the class, smiling, not missing a beat. Once every panelist had taken their turn to speak on the intricacies navigating the literary world, the professor dismissed everyone. Eli and Chase began packing their bags.

"Eli," Professor Fitzwilliam called out. "Come here for a minute."

Eli looked over at Chase and shrugged his shoulders. "I'll call you later to fill you in." Chase nodded, leaving the room.

As he started his way down to the front of the class, his professor continued. "I'd like to introduce you to Gianna Wickham. Eli is one of the brightest students we have in the class and is normally on time."

Eli gave a sheepish grin to the professor as he strode up reaching his hand out. The feeling of Gianna's hand was electrifying. It fit so well in his and the softness caught him off guard. "Pleasure to meet you, Ms. Wickham."

"Oh, please call me Gia. The only people I want calling me that are my clients and any bill collectors."

Eli laughed. "Very well, Gia." Eli let go of her hand, nervously running his hand through his hair. She intrigued him.

"Well, I'll leave you both to it," Fitzwilliam said. "I have a lunch appointment to attend and would like to stop by my office to drop my briefcase off."

"Thank you, Fitz, for putting something like this together. It was an amazing opportunity, not just for the students but for the panelists as well," Gia said.

"Oh, my pleasure, really," Fitz replied. "It is always nice to bring in powerhouses and have them talk to our green behind the ears students."

"I hope Darci is okay," she said.

"I'm sure she'll be alright. Though I thought she'd have been able to handle herself better."

"You expect too much from someone with little to give, Fitz."

Eli couldn't help but pick up on the unspoken elephant in the room. The three of them knew each other and something had happened. He would have to find out. Professor Fitzwilliam left the room, leaving just Eli and Gia to talk.

"So, I hear you have an internship at De Bourgh," Gia said in a friendly tone.

"I do. I leave here in a few weeks to go to New York."

"Are you well acquainted with Darci or any of the De Bourgh team?"

"I know Darci a little as we've had several run-ins," Eli paused, debating how honest he should be. "Most of them have been nightmares, if I'm being honest."

Gia's laughter echoed against the walls. It was infectious and light. "So you've been initiated into the Disgruntled Darci Club, I take it."

Eli chuckled. "Yes, I have. Where do I buy a shirt?"

"I'm afraid they aren't in print anymore, but I think I might have a spare in my suitcase."

"How much do you want for it?"

Gia put her hand on her chin, tapping it gently as if pondering a good price. Her finger flew up in the air. "How about lunch, or maybe dinner?"

Eli smiled. Her magnetic personality and beauty captivated him. He'd be up for both if she'd allow it. "Dinner?" Eli said.

"Perfect! Seven o'clock this Friday work for you?"

"At your hotel restaurant? Ya know, so I can get that shirt from you." Eli winked.

Gia flushed. Good, it wasn't just him feeling the connection.

"That works for me."

"I'll see you then."

The bus ride home Eli allowed various case scenarios explaining the bad blood between Gia and Darci to play out in his head. Every outcome seemed plausible to him, knowing firsthand how Darci was when interacting with other humans. He'd try to get the full story from Gianna when they had their date.

He made it home and set straight for the phone. It had been a few weeks since he and Chase had hung out, which was weird for them. He'd attempted to call Chase a few times but never could reach him and his grandmother had been little help. She never seemed to know where he was, which was even more odd.

Eli dialed Chase's number and stood waiting for the other end of the line to stop ringing. He wasn't much for answering machines and ended up rambling ninety percent of the time.

"Hello?"

"It's about time you answer my call," Eli said, feigning irritation.

"Pfft. I've just been busy, that's all."

"Busy doing what," Eli asked. "Your grandma wasn't exactly in the know."

"I've been helping to organize another equality march," Chase said. "Actually, I was going to see if you wanted to come over Saturday morning and come march with me."

Eli smiled. He loved that Chase helped to plan these sorts of powerful events and thought to invite him along. "I'd love to," Eli responded. "What should I wear?"

"I'd suggest something comfortable and a good pair of walking shoes."

"You got it. I'll be at your house around 7 am?"

"That's perfect," Chase said. "Okay, now spill the beans about your weekend."

"Strap in Chase, cause this was an entire journey."

Eli spent the next forty-five minutes giving Chase a play-by-play and fielding all questions he had. James still hadn't opened up to share much about what happened between Charleigh and him, and was still taking it easy. Of course, Chase also had to ask about what happened after he left the lecture hall. When Eli told him about walking away with a date, Chase lost his mind with excitement. If this was how people would react to him having a date, he didn't want to tell anyone else.

Chapter 13

Various scenarios explaining the bad blood between Gia and Darci played out in Eli's head. Every outcome seemed plausible to him, knowing firsthand how Darci behaved when interacting with other humans. He'd try to get the full story from Gianna tonight at dinner. He opened the door to his house, the silence surprising him. Unnerving was a better way to put it. Usually he'd hear the blathering of Mark or the tormented bickering between Kit and Lance.

"Hello?" Eli shouted as he shut the door behind him.

"Upstairs," a distant, muffled voice said in response.

Eli dropped his book bag down on the foyer floor and ran upstairs. The door to their room was open. James sat on the side of his bed staring at a crumpled up piece of paper. "What is that?" Eli inquired.

"A letter Charleigh wrote." His voice quivered as he pressed on. "They were called back to New York and they won't be coming back."

Eli slumped down next to James and took the letter from his hand, opening it up and straightening it out before reading it aloud.

James,

By the time you get this, Karl and I will be on our way back to New York. I don't think I'll be back in Meryton in the foreseeable future, and so I've listed Netherfield Park with a realtor. It was fun while it lasted, and you're by far my favorite fling. Thank you for everything.

Charleigh

Eli stood up, crumpling the paper as James had already done, throwing it into the trash can. "That's bullshit James."

"No, she was pretty clear," James said, looking down at his empty hands. "It was a fun fling."

"She cares for you!"

"And how do you know?"

"I saw her with my own eyes, looking at you in a way only someone who loves another does, while you were laid up in bed." Eli paced the room and ran his fingers through his hair. "People don't dote on someone like that unless they have an emotional attachment."

"To think I read her wrong this whole time," James said between sniffs. "I gave her the very best parts of me and even entertained thoughts of marriage."

"James, you did nothing wrong."

"I played the part of a fool, Eli," James said, looking into his brother's eyes. "Should've known someone like me wouldn't have a chance with someone like her." James flopped back onto the bed, staring at the ceiling.

"That's horseshit!" Eli roared. "If she's so vapid as to not understand that you're worthy of her attention, well, then she's the fool. Not you." He walked over to James' bed and flopped down on his belly, glancing at James. "I can stay in tonight and we can go drink our troubles away."

"Stay in? Did you have plans for tonight?" James looked over at him, curiously raising one eyebrow.

"I do, but I can cancel."

"Like hell you can." James turned to get a better look at Eli's face. "Who is she?"

"No one you know, but James, dear god James, I understand now the way you felt with Charleigh."

"Oh?"

"She is stunning." Eli lifted his hand to rest his head on. "But it isn't just her looks. She is a brilliant mind, funny, and just fun to be around."

"Sounds like you've finally struck gold," James chuckled. "I wouldn't dream of you missing your date on account of my shitty love life."

"Are you sure?"

"Absolutely. I'll get over this eventually and what if this girl ends up being something permanent and you miss your chance because of your cry baby big brother? I refuse to be the one that ruins a shot at possible bliss for you."

"You're getting ahead of yourself, James." Eli laughed.

"Maybe, but you never know," James paused for a moment before inquiring more. "What were you planning to wear?"

"Well, I was going to ask to borrow a suit of yours, if that is okay."

"Really wanting to impress this lady, aren't you?"

"I prefer to not look like a bum for our first date, yes."

"Good plan. Take whatever you need, Eli."

Eli wasn't much for the dating scene. His ambitions were greater than attempting to navigate the intricacies that was women. What he wanted in life just wasn't conducive to him settling into a relationship. The shower was the only spot in the house that allowed him clarity. However, today he received no helpful revelations, only a plethora of unanswered questions.

Where did he hope Gia and he would go, and did he want to invest for the first time in someone else outside his family? These questions hung in the air, tinged with dread and anxiety. He knew he'd leave for New York soon and that'd throw a wrench into things. A long-distance relationship was in the realm of possibilities for him if they hit it off, and he'd be okay with traveling when he could to visit her. It'd be all the better if she established her publishing house in New York City, too. He was getting preposterously ahead of himself.

"Date first," Eli mumbled to himself as he walked the rest of the way up to the hotel. He'd never been to this hotel. It was too high priced for anyone he knew to stay there, though word on the street was the restaurant was worth the money. Eli had a financial buffer for when he moved to New York City, enough to last until he got his first paycheck from De Bourgh, but felt this was a suitable time to reallocate funds.

Gold revolving doors opened to a foyer that glistened with crystals, marble, and gold trim. It smelled of old money and expensive cologne and perfume. A gentleman strode up to him, slightly bowing.

"Good evening, sir. How may I assist you?"

The formal greeting threw Eli off guard. "The restaurant?"

The tuxedo clad man jutted out his arm. "It would be this way, sir. Would the gentleman like an escort to the door?"

Eli had to hold back from bursting into laughter. What a wildly strange world this was. "No, thank you. I believe I can find my way there without your help."

"Very well, sir. I bid you a pleasant evening."

The whole interaction was stuffy and old mannered. With that in mind, Eli took in the people milling about the lobby and entrance to the restaurant. Pricey pretentiousness seemed to be the theme of the night, and he was sure he stuck out like a sore thumb.

He waded through the crowd of finely dressed women, who paid him no mind and continued to cluck away, to the host podium. Behind the stately wooden pillar stood a rigid man, white gloves skimming the book in front of him. "Name?"

"Ellington Bennet."

"I don't see a reservation under that name," the man eyed Eli, scrutinizing him. "I believe you might have made a reservation elsewhere."

"I was unaware that one needed a reservation here."

The man let out a gasp, offended at Eli's comment. "Excuse me, sir. We are a three Michelan star restaurant that serves the finest cuisine in the state and possibly the country. Polite society comes from all over the world to savor the delights that are Chef Dubois' masterpieces. To suggest such ignorance is an affront to this establishment."

Eli threw his hands up to calm the man down. "Look, I wasn't trying to be offensive. I'm set to meet a guest at the hotel here, but we'll just go somewhere else." The incessant need to bite back itched his brain. He needed to leave well enough alone, but it just wouldn't stop pecking at him. Eli gave into his impulse. "I wouldn't want to eat here, anyway. The taste of greed doesn't sit well. I end up on the shitter all day if I indulge." The revulsion on the man's twisted face satisfied him.

"Eli?" Gia's voice sweetly came from behind.

He turned around. Gia stood in front of him wearing a royal blue, figure-hugging cocktail dress. Her auburn hair swept up in a loose updo, ringlet curls framing her face. "You look," Eli cleared his throat before continuing, "breathtaking."

"Thank you. I could say the same for you." Her dazzling smile lit up the place. "Is there a problem?" Gianna glanced around Eli, making note of the concierge's face.

"How do you feel about *not* eating here?"

Gia laughed. "Sure, I guess."

Eli clapped his hands together, peering back at the incensed man, and gave a slight wave.

He reached out his hand, seeking Gia's. She took it and Eli led her through the sizable crowd that'd amassed.

"What was all that about?" Gia asked once clear of the crowd.

"I might have offended the man with my cave dweller ways," Eli said, the corner of his mouth tilting up in amusement.

"Cave dweller, you say," Gia teased.

"Yeah, and if we don't find some place to eat soon, it's only going to get worse."

Gia giggled. "Okay, where to?"

"Do you like Italian food?"

"It's my favorite."

"Great! There's a place around the block."

Once they ordered, Eli and Gia found a table in the corner, away from the bustle of the dinner rush. The small talk they'd had walking to the restaurant troubled Eli. A heaviness settled in his gut; his intuition telling him she hadn't been one-hundred percent forthcoming.

"So," Eli said, throwing his coat over the back of the chair. "What exactly brought you to Meryton?"

"As I told you," Gia pulled out her chair. Eli stared at the chair blankly, knowing full well he'd failed. Gia sat down and continued, "I'm trying to start my publishing company and so I'm traveling to a few locales to find the right space for my office."

"And what do you think of Meryton so far?"

"I think it's quaint and harkens back to Mayberry times." Gia laughed.

"I've never heard someone describe the town that way," Eli chuckled, "but it's on point."

"Thank you. I try my best!" Gia smiled.

"So, the tension in class today—" Eli paused as he saw the server coming to their table with their food.

"I have a deep dish three meat pizza?" The young man said, looking at Eli.

"That is actually the lady's." Eli grinned while pointing at Gia.

"Oh! Sorry about that," the server said as he sat the pizza in front of Gianna.

"It's okay," Gia said, waving it off.

"Supreme no black olives for you, sir?"

"Yep. Thanks!"

"Do you guys need anything else?"

Eli looked at Gia, who shook her head. "No. I think we're good."

"Great. Enjoy you guys."

As the server plodded off to attend another table, Eli picked up where he left off. "I assume something happened between you two to have cultivated the hostile environment?"

"Eli, you saw everything happen as I did." Gia took a piece of pizza off the tray, holding it in her hand. "The only person hostile in that room was Darci."

"That's fair."

"She just won't get over herself."

Eli took a bite of pizza, pondering his next words. He took a drink of his beer to wash the bite down and decided to just ask outright. "So, what is the history between you and Darci?"

"I don't want to badmouth her and prefer to keep the past in the past."

"I understand, however, I'll soon work with the woman. It'd be beneficial for me to know what I'm getting myself into."

Gianna took a sip of tea. Her lips pressed together in dismay while she stared into her glass, using the straw to stir the sugar that'd settled at the bottom, turning her cup into a snow globe. Her brows furrowed as she weighed her options.

"Look, I promise whatever you say stays between just you and I."

Gia lifted her head and nodded while gazing into Eli's eyes. "Well, Darci and I grew up together. My parents died when I was four years old in a car accident. Darci's dad took me in as my father worked for him as his groundskeeper."

"Sorry to hear that. I'm glad you had him looking out for you."

"Me too, honestly. I wouldn't be the person I am today if it wasn't for him. Anyway, as an only child, Darci was the closest thing I had to a sister and George, a brother. I lost two members of my family but ended up gaining two back."

"It seems like you guys got along then. So what happened?"

"We were best of friends until seven years ago when her father died." Gia slumped in her chair.

The look on her face reminded him of a beaten down animal. "That is a lot of loss for you to experience."

"It was rough, but I feel bad for Darci. Her mom died in childbirth with George, and her father never remarried. So she's never known what it feels like to have a mother's warmth in her life."

"That would explain some things."

"Exactly. I don't think she'll ever be good mom material because she lacks the ability to be selfless."

Eli sat back in his chair. The interactions he had with Darci fit with the narrative. He almost felt as though he was the asshole in all their interactions, but he pushed it out of his mind. She'd been rude since day one.

"What happened after Darci and George's father died?"

Gia let out a drawn-out sigh. "I was out of town on a business trip when I received the news. I found the first flight out, hoping to get there as soon as possible. There were massive delays all over the country because of a dangerous blizzard. I was stuck for days, unable to attend the funeral."

"Don't tell me that Darci faults you for not being there," Eli exclaimed incredulously.

"It certainly didn't help matters," Gia muttered, taking a drink of her watered down tea. "When I finally could fly in, I was informed that I wasn't allowed to enter the house." She leaned her elbow on the table, using it to prop her hand up to hold her chin. "Of course, I had no place to go, so I booked a room at a hotel outside of the city."

"You've got to be kidding me. Why the fuck could you not have entered your own goddamn home?" Eli asked, his voice rising as he found it harder and harder to control his anger.

"The will."

"Surely her father didn't write you out."

"Oh, he didn't. That's the problem."

A light bulb went off in Eli's head. Darci didn't believe she lay claim to any of her father's estate because they weren't blood related. "Good. That would've been a shitty thing to do, especially after you'd been a sister to them. What did George think of all this?"

"George is younger than Darci and I, so at the time he was off at boarding school and a minor. I didn't see fit to weigh him down with something he had no control over."

"So, what did he leave to you in the will?"

Gia looked Eli in the eyes. "A board seat for De Bough Publishing and a third of the control of the company."

Eli chewed in quiet disbelief. He threw down the slice of pizza and stood abruptly, unsure how to handle the information. Fury raged within. He ran his fingers through his hair, the other hand set on his hip. Fresh air. He needed fresh air.

"Eli," Gia called out after him. Her chair scraped against the floor as the door shut behind him. She ripped his jacket off the back of the chair and followed him out the door. "Hey, are you okay," she asked, handing Eli his jacket.

The deep cleansing breaths he took did nothing for the heat of his temper. "Yeah, I'm just fucking pissed for you. And to think I danced with that woman, allowed her to weasel her way into my good graces, let alone accepted an internship at that shitty fucking company."

"I shouldn't have said anything." Gia sighed. "I'm sorry."

"No. I asked, and you did the right thing." He knew there was a finale, as she wouldn't be looking for a place for her company headquarters. "Tell me the rest."

"Are you sure?" Gia looked at him, puzzled and worried.

"Yeah, I need to know all of it."

"Well, when the executor read the will, Darci found out that I had as much control over the company as her and George. She used her rights as George's legal guardian to oust me from the company. She bought me out, even though I was unwilling to sell, and left me on the wayside."

Silence screamed out after she finished telling the story. Eli wasn't sure where to go from there, but something had to be done.

"Gianna?"

"Hmmm?"

"Is there a way we can get you back what is rightfully yours?"

"I don't know that there is. The only way I could think to do that would be to take the company itself down, which would force the board to remove Darci."

"How do we do that?"

"Well, you have that internship, right?"

"Yeah."

"And you want to land a job as an investigative journalist?"

"That's the goal. Where are you going with this?"

"I have an idea, but I really don't want to drag you into all the drama."

"Listen, I'm a big boy. I can handle myself. The important thing is righting the wrongs."

"Okay. De Bourgh Publishing prides itself on being the biggest publisher in the nation," Gia took a deep breath before continuing. "What the world doesn't know, and they have pain-stakingly kept under wraps, is that they are nothing more than a vanity publisher that cons unsuspecting new authors into contracts that they can't possibly profit from or get out of."

"This just keeps getting worse." Eli grabbed Gia into his arms, holding her. "So this is what I will do. I will keep my plan to do the internship and with the access I get, I will gather proof and write up an investigative piece and aim to take down the company."

"Are you sure, Eli?" Gia asked, her arms wrapping around Eli, hugging him back.

"Absolutely. It could take a year, but I'll do it."

Chapter 14

T he cool of the night was a welcome retreat from the nausea that had welled up. He'd offered to do something that he wasn't entirely sure he could pull off. This would either destroy him or it would send him skyrocketing to the top levels of the journalism field. He had to be sure he did this right, as one misstep would annihilate him.

Eli chewed on potential ways to execute this while he walked home. He needed to talk this through with someone who'd be objective in the matter. He looked both ways before crossing the street and rerouted himself. The tightening in his chest grew with every step towards Chase's house. Dread settled in his bones with the realization that he'd once again allowed his emotions to dictate his actions.

In full sprint, Eli rounded the corner of Chase's street, clammy sweat beaded up on his forehead. Bile churned, forcing Eli to stoop over the grass next to him. He purged the burden and felt no lighter. Cinder blocks weighed him down as he took the last few steps to

Chase's door. Eli's head swam as he pounded on the door—breaths, sharp and ragged.

Eli turned his back to the front door, leaned against it, and slid down. He put his head between his legs and focused on breathing and pushing thoughts from his mind. When the door opened, Eli fell back.

"Eli," Chase bent down, wrapping his arms under Eli's armpits, attempting to hoist him up. "What happened to you?"

"The world is spinning," Eli said while exhaling.

"Let's get you off the ground and to the couch. Can you walk?"

"Honestly, I'm not sure. Chase—" Eli shifted his weight, trying to help his friend maneuver him. "I think I made a grave mistake."

"God, Eli. What did you get yourself into now?"

Eli looked Chase in the eyes before hanging his head. "You know how I shot myself in the foot with Darci?"

"Yes," Chase said through clenched teeth as he tugged Eli to the couch.

"It's so much worse than that."

Chase made it to the couch before he let go in shock. Eli fell forward, face planting the arm of the couch. "Ellington Bennet! What do you mean it's worse? How can someone screw up a date so badly?" Chase's voice squeaked with panic.

Eli rolled over, rested the back of his head on the couch arm and moved his hands to his face, rubbing them up and down. A part of him had hoped this was a nightmare and the action would be enough to wake him.

"Well?" Chase asked, his hands firmly placed on his hips as he peered at the sprawled out form on his couch. Eli sighed. "It didn't pan out?"

"The date isn't the problem, and I assure you. It went great." Eli shook his head at his lack of control. "I may have offered to do something that could be career ending."

"The hell do you mean by that?" Chase asked, staring incredulously at his friend.

"Gia told me about how De Bourgh and Darci wronged her." Eli ran his fingers through his hair. "I suggested I could help her seek retribution."

"You didn't!"

"I did."

"Eli, why would you throw your future on the chopping block for a person you barely know?"

"Look, at the moment, it seemed like the right thing to do. It could benefit her and I, but now I'm having some reservations."

"You know what this is? A classic case of a knight in shining armor syndrome." Chase flopped down next to Eli on the couch. "You always do this. Let your emotions get the best of you because of a morally wronged person with no thought to how this could bite you in the ass."

"What do I do?" Eli asked, looking over at Chase and furrowing his brow in desperation.

"I know what I'd do in this situation, but I also know what will win out, so there is no point in me offering my two cents."

"Wow. Thanks, Chase."

"I don't mean to seem unsupportive. It's just that you have a mind of your own and once it's made up, it's nearly impossible to talk you out of it." Chase crossed his arms over his chest and leaned back on the couch. "For you to go throw yourself to the proverbial wolves, it must be a damning slight against Gianna."

"It really is." Eli sat forward and rested his arms on his knees, clasping his hands and stared down at them. "And it's within my power to expose something much bigger than me and it could not only help Gia get back what she lost but it will prevent something like this from ever happening again."

"What do you need from me?"

"I don't know how to go about doing this," Eli said, inhaling deeply.

"So you are going to expose De Bourgh for wrongdoings via your internship?"

"Yeah."

"First things first. You need to go to New York to scope things out."

"Not sure what reason to come up with for a preemptive visit to De Bourgh though."

"You have family in Vermont, right?"

"An aunt and uncle in the Burlington area, yeah."

Chase uncrossed his arms, jumped up while simultaneously clapping his hands together. It was Chase's tell for having thought up a brilliant idea, which is exactly what he needed. "Okay, call them and see if they'd help guide you around New York. You can use the 'I need to prepare for my move' excuse."

"So I do that, and then what?"

"You do your due diligence with a visit to De Bourgh for a tour, and sight-see like a normal person who hasn't ever left town."

"That could work," Eli said, placing his finger over his lips and resting his chin on his hand as he let Chase's words sink in.

"You'd get a feel for how things operate there so you can come back and come up with a plan."

He stood up, walked to Chase, and hugged him. Never in the years that they'd been friends had Chase turned his back on him, even when he'd obviously been the idiot. At least now he had a semblance of a plan, which was more than he'd have on his own.

Chase pulled away, turning his head toward the dining room and then back at Eli. "Since you're here, you wanna help me make signs?"

Eli looked at Chase and nodded. "Point me in the direction, boss. If you're willing to put up with my shitty handwriting, lack of a creative bone in my body, and inability to write in a straight line, I'm game."

Chase chuckled. "Boy, you realize that this is for a gay march. I wouldn't accept anything less than a non-straight line."

Chapter 15

H is first flight ever taken was uneventful. The expectation he'd built up in his mind about being in a metal cage and floating in midair for a few hours had been more involved. He tried finishing *Pride & Prejudice* and to take notes for the essay that was due when he returned, though he still didn't know which direction he'd take the paper.

It'd seemed like they'd just gotten in the air by the time the pilot came over the over comm stating the expected weather in New York City, time, and thanking passengers for flying with them. He wasn't sure if it was nervousness about flying or the dry writing of Jane's, probably a bit of both, that caused him to read the same page repeatedly, but most of the two-hour flight he'd spent making little progress. Eli sighed, muttering obscenities under his breath. He had to make it through the book this week.

The plane taxied on the runway to its allocated spot and came to a stop. Everyone pushed themselves out into the aisle, making the sardine packed flying contraption look even more crammed. People fought to reach over one another's head to access their carry-on luggage from the bins above. It was an utter mess and one Eli was content in missing out on. He wasn't sure he could survive the fast pace of New York City.

Eli looked over at the man sitting next to him who'd been stooped for minutes, waiting for the right moment to make his great escape and join the masses scrambling about. He took a deep breath, opened the book back up and attempted to drown out the madhouse. Once most of the warm bodies had left, leaving only a few stragglers milling out of the plane, he got up and collected his stowed away items. His jaw relaxed and his shoulders fell once he was free from the metal prison.

Navigating the maze of LaGuardia wasn't as chaotic as he'd thought it would be. Crisp air filled Eli's lungs as he stepped through the sliding glass doors. A polyphonic blend of people chatting, sirens screaming, and cars honking made Eli cringe. He took in his surroundings and noticed the taxi attendant on the opposite side of the throng of people.

Eli pushed his way through and stopped at the back of the line, his ears trained on the conversations happening in front of him, striving to gather any helpful information on how to navigate and secure a taxi when it was his turn. Accents were thick yet varied, and some he struggled to understand. The line progressed rather fast, and it was now Eli's turn to attempt hailing his first cab.

"Where are you headed to," asked the lanky attendant.

The man's accent was hard to process. His baritone voice, along with the elongated vowels and dropped r's, added to Eli's auditory confusion. "I'm sorry. What?"

"I said, where to," the attendant said, slowing down and enunciating.

"Um, do you know where the King's Carriage House is?"

"Yeah, Upper East Side."

"Where is that?" Eli asked.

"It's a neighborhood in Manhattan."

"Okay. How does this work? Does it go by mileage or time?" Eli asked.

"From the airport to Manhattan is a flat fee of thirty dollars."

"Much more simple than I thought it would be." Eli cracked a grin.

"Alright," the man said, pointing to a yellow taxi in the middle of the long procession, and held out a receipt while peering around at the person behind him. "Next."

Eli looked from the taxi and back to the man who'd abruptly dismissed him and took the paper from his hands. The terseness of it all confused him. He'd no direction outside 'go to the pointed out car'.

"Bonjou," a jovial voice shouted out, waving him over to his car.

Eli attempted to process the jumbled words he'd just heard while making his way over to the now opened car door. It resembled French to his ears but was off somehow. He furrowed his brow as he put his carry-on bag in the backseat before sliding in next to it and shutting the door. The man sat down in the driver's seat and looked back, his round face smiling at Eli while staring expectantly at the paper he held in his hand.

"Do you need this?" Eli asked, holding out the paper.

"Yeah."

Eli gave him the slip of paper and sat back, moving his attention to the window. He tried to think back to the last time he'd seen his aunt and uncle. It'd have been Christmas 1985. 13 years seemed like only yesterday. He was a 10-year-old boy, watching the Saturday morning Transformers cartoons while playing with the new and highly sought after Optimus Prime Transformer he'd gotten three days before as a gift from them. They'd moved to Vermont the following spring and hadn't been down to visit since.

They kept in contact with postcards of their travels and phone calls, but life was busy, too busy to find time for Meryton kin. It was hard not to take it personally as a kid. Once he reached the age of reasoning, he realized it was less about him and more about them. They were off enjoying life, and he couldn't blame them. He'd dreamed of leaving his small town suburb of Atlanta and experiencing the world. That it would induce this level of anxiety never crossed his mind.

Parkas dotted the sidewalk. People milled around at the stoplights, collectively moving along the pavement. It was reminiscent of ants. They all traversed with purpose and fluidity to their ultimate destination, and this would be his new home for the foreseeable future.

The taxi slowed to a stop in the far right lane. "King's Carriage House for ya. Thirty dollars."

Eli reached into his back pocket for his wallet and took out two twenty-dollar bills. He'd done a bit of research before leaving on tourist etiquette and when dealing with taxi drivers' tips was a must. Though he never could figure out how much was acceptable. He placed the bills in the man's hand. "I hope that's enough of a tip. I don't know what I'm doing here."

The driver smiled, glanced down at the two folded bills in his hand, and nodded. "This is good. Thank you."

"Have a great rest of your day." Eli opened the door and scooted his way out, turning to grab his carry-on, and gave a small nod while shutting the door. As the taxi drove off, all he could do was stare at the looming wall of red bricks in a sea of concrete. The large window, with wrought iron decorative shutters, gave a view of the classical furnishings and embellishments. The opulent Beaux-Arts manor, dregs of a lost era, stuck out like a sore thumb amongst modern architecture. Two stories of sheer aristocratic atmosphere left him in a state of awe.

He moved through the door, scanning the surroundings. Gilded paintings, crystal chandeliers, and antique furniture complimented the light goldenrod yellow walls with dark mahogany trim. Round tables sporadically stippled the room, decorated with mismatched china tea sets and three tiered pewter trays. Each tray held random smatterings of finger foods. He knew time travel was impossible, but this certainly made him question reality.

"Eli!" An excited, familiar voice called. "We're over here."

Eli looked over and saw his aunt wildly waving her arms, an enormous smile plastered across her face. Next to her, staring down at the miniature sandwich on his plate, was his uncle. The disappointment etched into his face made him chuckle. This had to have been his aunt's idea. "Hey, Marina," Eli said as he made his way through the table maze.

His aunt pushed back her chair, standing up, arms spread and ready for a hug. Eli wasn't much of a hugger, but for those he loved, he would sacrifice. He dropped his bag next to an open chair and hugged her.

"How was the trip," his uncle asked, his face not leaving his plate.

"It was good. How was you guys' trip?"

Edward lifted his face from his plate, making eye contact with Marina. "It went fairly well, though had I known this was our first destination, I'd have stopped on the way at McDonald's."

"Ed, you'll be fine. We'll get you a burger for dinner," Marina shot back. "Eli, sit. I'll find our server." Marina went over to a little nook in the wall where they were standing and pointed to the table they were sitting at.

"Not your cup of tea?" Eli quipped. He couldn't help himself. Edward looked up at Eli, letting a moment pass before giving in to the fit of laughter he'd tried to hold in.

Marina made it back to the table and looked her husband up and down, perplexed. "What did I miss?"

"Nothing much. Eli over here is rather witty. I think he gets that from me."

"Don't flatter yourself," Marina said with a grin.

It was nice catching up with them over finger sandwiches and tea. He had to admit while this wasn't his thing, the experience was fun. They took him to their hotel, letting him get cleaned up before heading out to sight-see. It worked out well since Eli was still needing to get a hotel room and preferred to be near family, just in case.

While Edward was involved in trade, he relished sharing his infinite knowledge of architecture, something he had studied since he was a boy. This was his moment to shine. Their first stop was to the Woolworth building, which Eli found out was one of the earliest American skyscrapers and the tallest building until nineteen thirty. After that, they stopped by the Chrysler building, Empire State building, Flatiron building, St. Patrick's Cathedral, and ended at Central Park. The only thing running through Eli's mind while listening to his aunt and uncle prattle on about each landmark was how much he missed home.

Eli decided he didn't want to wait til tomorrow to visit De Bourgh Publishing. The building was only a few blocks away from where they were at Central Park and it was only four o'clock in the afternoon. A quick tour would allow him to get the annoyance of introductions out of the way.

Chapter 16

C lad in a wall of black steel and green-tinted glass, with darker glass spandrel panels separating each of the 77 levels, De Bourgh Publishing disappeared in the curtain of smog and low-lying clouds above. He was in the beast's belly and it made his skin crawl. Greed and selfishness of corporate America ruled this domain. It was the reason he wanted to get into journalism in the first place, and now he'd work for a company that thrived off taking advantage of those looking to gain a foothold in life.

Eli moved solemnly through the doors, his chest constricting. Tension infiltrated his muscles, making it difficult to put one foot in front of the other. Sound faded around him as he took in the grandiose and over done lobby area. Suits moved past him uniformly towards one singular gathering point. The elevators, dealing in the transportation of lost souls, moved with ease up the damning tower. His collared blue plaid button up and favorite pair of jeans, light and worn, singled him out from the monochrome masses.

The ding of the elevator ripped him out of the uncomfortable trance he'd hidden away in. Everyone moved in the car in seamless fashion, leaving him as an obvious outsider. Eli stepped in last, looking at the slew of lit up numbered buttons on the panel next to him. This would undoubtedly be the longest elevator ride of his life. A sigh escaped his lips as the door opened for the first stop. He'd have to get used to this as soon it would be his every day.

"Excuse me," a voice rang out right before the force of someone pushing past caught Eli off guard. He reached out instinctively to steady himself, his hand landing square on the control panel, lighting up more buttons. Collective groans and aggressive mumblings filled the silent void. Eli wanted to disappear from the eyes he felt bore into the back of his head.

He watched the floor numbers tick by slowly. Luckily for him, the rest of the ride to the 27th floor was mundane. The elevator door opened to a large foyer. Eli stepped out and took a deep breath as he digested the atmosphere. Shiny white marble flooring reflected a large antique bronze De Bourgh Publishing sign that hung on the wall behind the semicircular receptionist desk. To the right was a line of plush black leather seats that were positioned in front of the glass cases, filled with books, lining the walls.

"Can I help you?"

Eli looked at the woman, and rubbed his palms on his jeans, hoping to dry the sweat that'd built up from the nerve-racking elevator experience. "Hi, yeah. I'm Ellington Bennet."

"Okay, Mr. Bennet, how can I help you?"

"I'm starting an internship here soon and was hoping to get a tour of the company."

"An internship?" Suspicion edged her tone. "Please hold, while I verify this with Mr. De Bourgh."

"Yeah, no problem," Eli said, shoving his hands in his pockets and strolling to the wall of books. Aged leather bound spines spoke to his soul. Many of the books looked to be first edition prints of literary greats. The likes of James Joyce, F. Scott Fitzgerald, and John Steinbeck were among the myriad of authors represented.

"How do you like our homage to our imprint library?" Eli spun around on his heels towards the voice and watched as the silver haired older man walked towards him. A hand reached out to Eli, who responded in kind, and gave it a firm shake. "I'm Keats. My niece told me you might come up to visit and get familiar with your new home. How have you found things?"

"Well, sir, overwhelming."

Keats let loose a deep belly laugh. It was unnerving to see another one of Darci's relatives be so genial. It confused him even more why she was the way she was. "Let's get started, Mr. Bennet." Keats signaled to the door by the receptionist's station.

"Please call me Eli."

Keats looked him over and nodded. "Alright, Eli. I'll show you to your desk first and then move on from there."

Eli walked through the door first, with Keats following behind. The room opened up to strategically placed cubicles. Glass walls lined the room, each an office of someone undoubtedly important to the company. Clacks hollered out from mechanical keyboards, infusing the atmosphere with melody between hushed murmurs.

"This is the pit, where we have editors and agents working on submissions," Keats said, nodding his head over to the far left glass wall. "And that over there is the conference room."

"So what is the process like for submissions?"

"Oh, it's fairly simple. We've a team of agents and editors who are assigned to each main genre category. They filter through the submissions, reading through them to see if they are worth the company's time."

"How do you determine what is worth the company's time?"

"Ah, that is a good question." Keats whistled loudly and the sounds of the room fell silent. "Gavin, come here for a second."

A slender polished man stood up from being hunched over a desk, adjusted his tie and suit jacket, before walking over to meet them. His navy suit was crisp, freshly pressed and his dark tan leather soled dress shoes gave a dull reflection of the fluorescent lights above.

"Afternoon, Keats," Gavin said.

"Afternoon. Gavin, this is Ellington Bennet. He will be our new intern for the Spring semester."

Gavin reached his hand out to Eli who took it, giving it one firm shake before letting go. "Welcome to the team."

"Gavin's in charge of making sure all departments follow the same protocols and operate smoothly," Keats said, looking at Eli before glancing back at Gavin. "Eli here was curious what the submissions process is like and thought you'd be the best to explain it."

Gavin nodded and looked at Eli. "So, our first step in sorting through submissions is looking to make sure they followed submission guidelines. If they don't, they're automatically rejected."

"How many get rejected just based on that alone?"

"We probably filter out a couple hundred a day."

"Wow, that's a lot."

"It's not our fault writers can't read," Gavin said, chuckling.

Eli struggled to keep a straight face. It was hard to fight back the impulse to unleash unfiltered insults Gavin's way, since he was a writer himself. Clearly, Gavin saw himself as a superior being, and he wondered how many others in this office held themselves in such high regard. "Right," Eli said, hoping the disdain he felt didn't seep through.

"After that, we see what the genre is and hand it off to the right team, who then will scan the piece looking for red flags, such as overdone tropes and ideas. Those get a basic form letter sent back to them." Gavin looked back towards the person who he'd been with moments before. "Fannie was actually asking me about a piece that was borderline automatic rejection."

"So you reject some not based on their writing ability, but rather because the market is too saturated with specific kinds of stories?"

"Basically. Then the ones that make it through get attention from our editors who look at the structure of the work. If it is a sound piece of work, they will send a revision request with markups."

The entire process sounded apathetic towards writers. People gave of themselves, time and energy, to write a story that spoke their heart. The fact they weren't given the time of day unless the powers-that-be deemed them worthy was disconcerting. How many future best sellers got ignored because of simple mistakes or ignorance?

Eli nodded his head as he glanced around the room at all the busy bodies moving between desks and chatting on the phones. "How long has the company been around?"

Keats ambled down the right side of the walls, prompting Eli to follow. A young woman in a taupe pantsuit needed Gavin's attention. "We were founded in 1813, eight generations ago by an uncle who felt *The Statesman* didn't do patrons justice. His vision was to provide relevant information in mass via compiling manuals into books."

"Seems like it started out as a benevolent effort on your distant relative's part."

Keats paused and glared at Eli. "Yes, I suppose it was." He resumed walking, stopping at the corner office and opening the door. There was a vertical partition wall separating out a simple desk from a larger desk behind the wall. "This is your desk and where you will report to."

Eli leaned in to get a view of the larger office. "Whose office is that?"

Keats turned back around to exit the room. "That's Darci's."

"Better and better," Eli muttered under his breath, rolling his eyes.

The rest of the tour was short and sweet. Keats' demeanor had changed from open and approachable to cold and distant. He'd have to figure out how to unfuck this before coming back. Eli was self-aware enough to know that he had a habit of making his life harder, and he hated it.

As they circled back to the door that led to the lobby, Eli's ears perked up when he overheard the name Bennet. Gavin and a familiar face, Karl, now had his attention. He slowed his pace to hear as much of the conversation as possible.

"Your sister should count herself lucky to have a friend like Darci," Gavin said, disgust smeared on his face. "Can you imagine having some backwoods hillbilly in your family line?"

Eli's fists balled up as he kept walking; his head held high. The gossip quieted down as he moved past them, only to pick up where they left off after he moved further out of their vicinity. So, the letter was Darci's doing. None of it surprised him.

He couldn't get out of the building fast enough. Anxiety melted into pure, fiery rage. The more he learned about Darci, the less he cared about anything she or her family offered. Internship or not. The rest of the time spent in the city was tarnished for him. All he wanted to do was go home and wash himself clean of the grotesque superiority he'd unwittingly bathed in.

Chapter 17

Eli paused mid towel dry, side-eyeing the envelope that'd been pushed under his door. He let out a sigh, walked over, and picked it up. It lacked any outward markings that would identify the sender. What looked back at him after he opened the shroud was a folded piece of gold embossed cardstock. The inked calligraphy confused him. He was positive that he'd found himself on Keats' shit list, but this invitation to his private residence for dinner tonight said otherwise. It even listed his aunt and uncle as guests.

Keats would send a black car to retrieve them at five o'clock sharp that evening and he was to wear his best dress. Eli sighed, looking at the open suitcase on his bed. He'd not thought to steal one of James' suits this go around. There was only one way to fix this dilemma: shopping. God, he hated shopping. Thankfully, his aunt was there and could help him reach *GQ* model status pronto. He hurried to his suitcase, discarding the invitation on the bed, and pulled out a black t-shirt and light wash jeans. There was so much to do and very little time. Not knowing where anything was in this city complicated matters.

Muted sounds of back-and-forth conversation through the hotel door let him know Marina and Ed were awake. Eli rapped on their door until he heard it unlock. He was flustered and beside himself, borderline needing a paper bag.

Marina opened the door. "Eli, are you okay? You look pallid," she said, placing the back of her hand on Eli's forehead.

"Mr. De Bourgh has invited us to a black tie dinner."

"Oh! How fun!"

"Marina, can I sit this one out?" Ed pleaded.

"Not a chance! Besides, how will it look if we don't go to support our nephew?"

Edward muttered unintelligibly under his breath.

"When is the event, Eli? Hopefully, we are here for it."

"Tonight. Keats is sending a car to collect us at five."

"Lord have mercy. That doesn't give us much time," Marina said, looking at her watch. "It's already nine thirty! We have only seven hours." She looked back at Edward. "Did you pack anything suitable, honey?"

"Heavens no. Why would I?" Edward grumbled. "This was not part of the plan."

Marina looked back to Eli. "Okay. So we need to find a store to get you both a suit and me a dress," she paused, looking Eli over. "And we need to get you cleaned up and a haircut. This disheveled look won't do."

"What's wrong with my look," Eli asked, offended.

"You scream college student, and well, that will not do. The middle part and longer hair might work back home, but you need to update your look."

After speaking to the concierge, they started on their journey. Luckily for them, they were in a central location near clothing shops and a barber shop. Paying for a suit wasn't in Eli's budget, but he'd have to suck it up and grab more cash from the ATM.

It took everything in him to not run away at his aunt's incessant need to look at every rack in the store. She was determined to leave no suit or dress unturned. The chattering between her and the sales associate made his eyes cross. They'd filled his arms with various jackets, pants, belts, and had thrown shirts over his shoulder. It was maddening.

"I think I've got enough things to try on," Eli said flatly.

Marina waved him on. As soon as the dressing room door latch clicked, he plopped down, resting his face in his hands. He didn't give one fuck what he wore. He lifted his head and ran a hand down his face as he took in the mound of suits and suit accessories. One by one he sorted through the mess, discarding obvious abominations he'd not be caught dead in. Only three suits made the cut. He'd try the three on and take whichever fit best. Thirty minutes later, he made his way out of the dressing room with one suit, shirt, and belt. He was done.

"Which one did you pick?" Marina asked, moving over to look at his choice. Her eyes widened slightly. "I suppose that'll do."

Eli followed his aunt to the checkout counter and handed the sales clerk the items. She quickly rang them up and looked at him. "That will be six hundred thirty-eight dollars and eighty-three cents."

He clenched his jaw and scowled. "Do you take a check?"

"Yes, sir."

The cost was over three weeks' worth of pay at the Meryton Press. His stomach twisted. None of this was what he wanted, yet he felt obligated to do it for Gianna and all the unsuspecting victims at the hands of Darci and company. If he had to suffer being down over six hundred dollars and a haircut, then it was a small price to pay. He only had to make it through the evening. What could go wrong?

Chapter 18

The collar of his shirt, cinched tight by the satin black tie, made it hard for him to breathe. Every time he'd worn one of his brother's suits, it'd been more comfortable. Padded-shoulders made him feel like he was playing high school football again while the double button part of the jacket looked absurd to him. His aunt and uncle were doing better than he was dealing with the situation.

After driving for forty minutes, the black town car pulled into a gated property. Warm, flickering glows from rich and ornate bronze sconces attached to the waist-high stone wall lit their way up the driveway. Around the bend in the pavement was a four tiered illuminated stone fountain surrounded by short hedges, highlighting the sprawling white limestone and marble three story chateau behind it. It was a masterpiece left by the bygone Gilded Era. He'd seen nothing like it in his life.

They pulled around to the front of the mansion, stopping between the split stone staircases. Renaissance inspired archways lead into a small balcony in front of the main entrance. Similar sconces lit the way up the stairs.

"Have you ever in your life—" Marina said, her jaw dropping in awe.

"If I'd known this was a surefire way to shut you up, I'd have brought you here long ago," Edward quipped.

The driver had already gotten out and opened their door. Eli slid out, moving to the side so the rest of his party could exit. He adjusted his tie and suit jacket, tugging on his shirt sleeves. He rotated his cufflinks, remembering the last time he wore any at all. It had been at the Masquerade ball almost a month ago, which was more so his element. Here he felt like a fish in the open water swimming amongst sharks.

Eli took a deep breath, letting it out as he started towards his destination. There was no turning back now. He put one foot in front of the other, climbing the steps, inching toward the great unknown. The click of Marina's high heels reassured him he wasn't alone.

A heavy and overly embellished door opened as Eli approached. The older gentleman gave a slight bow before moving his arm to the side showing the new guests in. "Good evening gentlemen and madam. How shall I announce you?"

"Announce me?" Eli asked, puzzled.

Marina stepped forward. "Mr. Ellington Bennet and Mr. and Mrs. Edward Gardiner."

"Very well." The man shut the door behind them and walked towards two closed arched doors.

"Haven't you ever seen any period dramas? Lord bless," Marina whispered to Eli as they followed the man.

"I'm sorry. I didn't think I would visit royalty on this trip. Had I known, I'd have better prepared," Eli snarked back.

Light airy notes sung out as the older gentleman pulled open both of the dark mahogany doors. Eli's eyes scanned the crowd, his attention stopping at the center of the room as light glinted off the swaying and spinning movements of sequined dresses. The twinkling gave the night sky a run for its money. The last movement rang out, followed by the bows and curtseys. Men held the hands of their partners, moving them off the polished hardwood floor.

"Announcing Mr. Ellington Bennet and Mr. and Mrs. Edward Gardiner."

Eli looked back at the man. It startled him to hear the once meek sounding voice morph into a booming force. The elderly man moved to the side, allowing Eli space to step through the doorway. Eli hated being the center of attention and the many pairs of eyes watching his every step unnerved him. They were all unfamiliar. He knew he'd be out of his depth here, but it wasn't until this moment that he felt the weight of societal differences tug at him, threatening to sink him.

A clap echoed off the walls. "Ah, you made it! Welcome to Rosings Park." Keats strode up to Eli, extending his hand out, which Eli took, giving it a brief shake. "How'd you find the trip here?"

Eli cleared his throat. "Fine." Marina kicked the back of his shoe's sole, sending Eli's head in a tizzy to find more words. "Though it was a beautiful drive and your house is stunning." Eli tugged again on his sleeve, trying to steady his nerves.

"Fantastic! Hang on." Keats walked away into the crowd, returning a moment later with a young and sickly looking man at his side. "Eli, I'd like to introduce you to my son, Andrew De Bourgh."

"Pleasure to meet you, Eli." His voice weakly cracked.

"Nice to meet you too, Andrew."

"Andrew here would have been top of his class had his health allowed him to be present more at Harvard. Not only that, he is proficient at anything he touches: piano, horseback, business matters, art. He is beyond reproach."

"I'm sorry to hear that," Eli said, looking at Andrew, forcing himself to swallow down the lump of pompous disgust that had formed in the back of his throat, replacing it with genuine concern. He never handled blatantly pretentious bragging well, and he hoped his irritation at Keats didn't trickle down to the undeserving new acquaintance.

"It's okay. I still graduated in the top twenty percent," Andrew said, shrugging his shoulders.

"Eli, Andrew, please excuse me. I need to go make a couple of announcements while the music has stopped." Keats moved past Eli and began making his way to the platform, stopping briefly to speak with various guests.

"So, you're the new intern? My father seems to have high hopes for you. Hopefully, you handle yourself better than the last intern did."

Eli shot a glance at Andrew, trying to decipher the cryptic comment, but hearing his name mentioned through the stage microphone stole his attention. "Come up here for a moment," Keats called out to him.

Andrew began clapping, causing the rest of the room to follow suit. Eli gingerly strode up to the stage, only stopping to meet outreached hands. His shoulders tensed to prepare for being put on the proverbial social chopping block. It was clear this was his first foray into the elite's inner circle. One he didn't fully expect and was unprepared to deal with. All he could do was pray that he wouldn't be required to speak. Brevity was not his strong suit when put on the spot.

"I officially would like to introduce you to De Bourgh's newest addition, Mr. Bennet." Keats clapped his hand on Eli's shoulder and looked at him, an inscrutable grin spreading across his face. "He comes to us all the way from Meryton, Georgia! Let's show him what makes De Bourgh the best company in the nation to work for."

Chapter 19

Dull throbbing pain settled into Eli's temples. The thought of having to go back into the chaos that was undoubtedly waiting for him added to his agitation. Frigid air that caressed his face did nothing to squash the knots in his stomach. It'd only been two hours since he'd arrived and he had at least another two more before he could escape.

Marina, as usual, worked the room with her charm. She made it look effortless, and he had to admit to being rather covetous of her abilities. His uncle found a pleasant corner to tuck himself into and get his fill of scotch and hors d'oeuvres. They both were of little help to him. He'd thought having them along would help ease the tension of being in an unknown environment with a plethora of elites.

The fall of footsteps ended his solitude. Eli turned to see the beaming smile of a young woman dressed in a flowy floor-length gown. Her dark waves rested on her shoulders.

"Sorry to intrude," she called out, continuing to make her way to him on the balcony.

"No intrusion," Eli lied. "I was about to come in. Needed some fresh air."

A spirited laugh filled the air. "No doubt the likes of curious and judging minds have inundated you since you walked through the door."

Her keen awareness and observation of his plight dragged a small grin across his face. "Will it let up at all tonight?"

"Doubtful," she giggled out. "I'm Kate, Darci's cousin." Kate reached her hand out to shake his.

Eli happily obliged. "I'm sorry."

"For what?" Kate asked inquisitively.

"For the relation."

"Oh!" Kate laughed. "Yes, she can be a bit of a ball buster, can't she?"

"From what I've seen, 'bit' is a reserved evaluation."

"Well, she is my cousin after all, though I'm not neglectful enough to argue against the truth." Kate gave a wink. "My uncle asked me to come get you for dinner."

"Your uncle is hard to read, but I think he hates me."

"Oh, he hates everyone. It's just the way of it," Kate said, matter of fact like.

"Makes me wonder who or what crawled up his ass."

"I don't know, but I don't think they make plungers big enough."

Eli let out a roar of laughter. This was the first time since he'd been in New York that he felt like he was connecting to someone real. It was a treat and one he hoped he'd have the honor of experiencing more often now.

"What's so funny?"

Laughter faded away abruptly. He knew that voice.

"Oh, nothing. I finally met the amazing Eli Bennet, and he did not disappoint." Kate turned to look at Darci, who was striding towards them.

Eli remembered the pain in his temples and rubbed them, praying for a release from it. It was a matter of time before this tension headache went full steam into a migraine with the bonus of a new pain—in the ass. He wouldn't allow her to think she'd gotten the best of him already.

"Evening, Darci." There. Short, sweet, and to the point.

"Good evening, Eli."

"My heavens," Kate said. "I can cut the tension with a paperclip."

"Oh hush, MacGyver." Eli caught a small twinkle in Darci's eye as the quip landed squarely on Kate.

"I see you've found the last bottle of bitch juice from Keats' private stash," Kate said. Her eyes level to Darci's and were equally alight.

"Don't be so crude, Kate. It's unbecoming."

"Ah, well, my dearest cousin, I'm not held to your 1950s charm school standards. Not since I firmly took my place as the black sheep by swearing an oath."

"An oath?" Eli asked.

Darci looked over at Eli and back at Kate. "Kate here spurned the family business in favor of terrible food, smelly men, and people barking orders at her."

"I took an officer position in the Army because," Kate looked back at Darci. "Surprise, surprise, I didn't like feeling purposeless in life."

Darci frowned and turned to Eli. "Keats told me to come find you both as Kate failed to return with you."

"I wouldn't say I failed." Kate chuckled.

"What would you say?"

"I'd say I was busy making a new friend." Kate grinned at Eli.

"Either way, everyone is waiting for our guest of honor before being seated."

"Fine," Kate said, reaching down and hooking her arm through Eli's. "Let's go give them something to talk about, shall we?"

Eli placed his free hand on hers. "With you by my side, I think we might do just that." Kate might be his only solace and reprieve from the antics of the evening.

A verbal sound of disgust echoed behind him, though he did his best to ignore it and focus on having a good time. The fact Darci had even made a sound in response to his and Kate's comments to each other bothered him. Who was she to think she had any right or say over who he talked with?

Chapter 20

An annoyed groan escaped Eli's lips as he turned over in bed to look at the bedside alarm clock. Six thirty in the morning. His mind had run through nightmare inducing thought minefields throughout the night. Sleep had been slow to come and hard to keep within his grasp. He flopped back over and stared at the ceiling, running through the events of the party for the fiftieth time. The realization that he was an outsider to this world, and he'd always be one, hurt. There was no place for him. Kate made it clear in her actions, leaving her birthright behind to find acceptance. If she couldn't make it in the dynamic, being raised within the confines of the elite, there certainly was no way he'd be able to. Luckily, he only had a few hours left before he'd be traveling back home.

He was brimming with excitement at the prospect of getting back into routine. Reinvigorated, Eli got up and collected the small suitcase he'd borrowed from James, filling it when a small knock rang out. He didn't expect his aunt to be awake this early, but she was his ride to the airport and maybe she knew something he didn't know about how long the process would take to get checked in and through security.

"I'm coming!" He flung the door open and immediately regretted it. "You're not Marina."

"I'm afraid not. Were you expecting her?"

"Yeah."

"I'm sorry to show up like this, but I need to speak with you—if that's okay." Darci attempted to hide the flushed pink that was creeping up her neck with her hand.

Eli had thought nothing of it and stood before her in a pair of old gray sweatpants, barefoot and shirtless. She was supposed to be his aunt, so he didn't at all feel bad for making her uncomfortable. She deserved to be uncomfortable.

"You wouldn't have any ideas about this James and Charleigh thing, would you?" Eli crossed his arms and leaned against the door-jamb.

Darci looked at Eli, setting her chin. "I prefer to keep that between the two of them."

"Well, then I'm afraid I can't help you." Eli stood back up straight, taking a step back, grabbing the door to shut it.

Darci's hand jutted out, forcing the door to halt. "Listen, can I please talk to you?"

Eli rolled his eyes. He knew he needed to entertain her because of the internship. "Fine." Eli opened the door wide again, inviting her in.

"Thank you," Darci said, moving past him; her sweet perfume wafting up to his nose.

Eli turned and shut the door, standing in the opening to the room. Darci moved around, her fingers twisting as she took in the open suitcase, shaking her head and nodding, though no sound came from her lips. The internal argument she was currently having with herself made being there watching awkward as hell.

"Darci?"

She shot her head over to look at him. "Hmmm. Oh, ummm—"

"Look, I have a busy day today. I have to pack."

"Pack?"

"Yes. I leave to go home today. I've done everything I needed to do to prepare myself for moving here."

"Right. Okay. Well." Darci paced back and forth wildly before stopping abruptly, looking at Eli. "Damn it, Eli. I must confess how much I care for you." She resumed her pacing before continuing. "I know that your station in life is well below my own and your family, well, they aren't exactly what I'd call respectable, though nice enough," Darci sighed. "I know this goes against the wishes of my family and my better judgment, but I can't hold this in anymore." Darci paused, looking at Eli, who was staring at her, eyes wide and slackjaw.

She waited a bit to see if he'd anything to say before moving on. Silence filled the air. She nodded. "Right, I'll continue," she said. "From the first time I met you at the Netherfield party, I've been fighting back the urge to not know you better. Our acquaintance, while fraught, I've enjoyed and as time has passed, it's led to me further admiring you as a person." Darci walked over to Eli, stopping a couple of feet away, looking into his eyes. "I'd very much like to put my heart at rest by asking you if you'd consider," Darci cleared her throat, "consider going on a date with me."

Eli felt like a bomb had gone off in that room. He couldn't make any words come out of his mouth. All he could do was stare, flabbergasted and silent. Of all the people in the world that could have announced their feelings like this, Darci was the last he'd have ever imagined doing so. This admission blindsided him. He'd been positive they'd held a mutual disdain for each other. It now appeared he was wrong, and it was a one sided street.

"Eli," Darci pleaded, "can you please say something? Anything?"

He didn't know how best to respond. Frankly, some of it pissed him off. He was balancing precariously on the precipice of unfettered anger and shock. If he were to open his mouth right then, there'd be no telling which way things would go. Yet she stared at him, waiting for a reply. Eli sighed, placing one hand on his hip, and the other ran down his face in bewilderment. It'd have to be the truth, and he resented her for placing her own pride in place of genuine affection. It was about how she felt and what others would think of her with zero regard for his own feelings. "Darci, I don't know what to say to all of that. I never once asked for your opinion and you've given it." Eli took a step closer, glaring at Darci. "I'm sorry to have sent you mixed signals if I did. It wasn't my intention at all."

"So, I pour my heart out to you and this is all you say?" Darci's voice raised in defiance.

"Oh, you want me to say more?" Eli shouted. "You profess you care about me, yet you throw my family under the bus and, to make things worse, insult me by stating you are going against your own judgment. You've given me no reason in the world to exalt you, and I'm inclined to credit you with breaking up Charleigh and James."

"You're right in your assumption. I worked to separate my best friend from your brother. I saved his heartache, unlike myself."

"Assumption?" Eli spit out. Appalled, he crossed his arms over his bare chest. "I heard it with my own two ears! It became water cooler talk at your own company, but that's not the only issue I have with you. Let's talk about Gianna Wickham and the disgusting behavior you showed to her. The disrespect of your father's wishes, let alone displacing someone who you grew up with as a sibling. What do you have to say about that?"

"You're eager to throw all your eggs in her basket."

"And why wouldn't I when she's been so horribly wronged, which aligns with the past track record of your behaviors I've witnessed with my own eyes?" Eli couldn't keep himself from yelling anymore. He'd gone past the point of no return and there would be no stopping him from ripping into her.

"Oh, yes—" Darci retorted with a sneer. "She was oh so wronged." Darci rolled her eyes.

"So now you mock her in front of me, knowing all of this is because of you!"

Darci turned from Eli, walking to the window, pulling back the curtain and staring out into oblivion. "All of this is what you think of me," she said, allowing the curtain to fall back into place and strode past Eli towards the door, turning back to continue. "If all of what you said is true about me, then, yes, my flaws are formidable. To think your ego is so fragile that my admittance to the misgivings and blatant truths have hurt you is laughable. I refuse to pretend to be someone I'm not and I'll not hide behind facades." Darci let out a bitter laugh, shaking her head. "You expect me to jump for joy at the fact that you're from the other side of the tracks, so to speak, knowing full well the implications of our world's colliding?"

"Allow me to thank you, before I show you the way out, for behaving like you did. If you'd been nicer, I might've had a harder time rejecting you. From the very beginning, I knew you were someone I would never want in my life." Eli walked to the door, grasping the handle and turning it, pulling it open. "I solely put up with you because I love my brother and his happiness was more important than my suffering in your company. Seeing as though you took care of that for me, I'm afraid there is no reason to have you in my life outside of the title: Boss." The icy stare Eli gave sent shivers down Darci's spine.

"You don't need to say anything else. I understand your hatred of me and I'm ashamed of my own feelings for you. Forgive me for wasting your time. Goodbye, Eli."

As soon as Darci moved through the doorway, Eli slammed the door behind her. "The fuck was that?" Eli shook his head, baffled.

Chapter 21

S weet, earthy odors of home refreshed his senses. The concrete jungle was behind him. Eli walked out of the airport as Chase's car pulled up, ripping Eli from his thoughts. He opened the back door and placed the suitcase on the seat.

"Hey," Eli said before shutting the door and opening up the passenger side door, sliding in.

"Hey yourself," Chase retorted.

"I see you're still as plucky as ever." Eli laughed out.

"It's not like you've been gone for months or even years."

"Well, it certainly felt like it."

"I take it, things didn't go as planned."

"They went as well as expected while being surrounded by headless people."

"Headless people?" Chase asked, turning on his blinker and pulling away from the loading zone.

"Yeah. All their heads are up their asses."

"So they need an assholectomy?"

Eli burst out in laughter. He'd missed Chase. It didn't matter what mood he was in, Chase always could pull him out of the darkness. "Enough about my shit. What's gone on in your world? It's been a hot minute since we've been able to catch up."

"Sorry, I've been really busy, but I have some news."

"Oh?"

"You will not like it."

"What gives you that idea?"

"I dropped out of school."

"You what?!"

"See, I knew you'd react this way." Chase chuckled, checking his mirror to merge into the fast lane.

"I was only gone for a week! How did you implode your life in a week?"

"Don't be dramatic, Eli." Chase relaxed his hand on the wheel, peering straight ahead.

"I'm not being dramatic." Eli gritted his teeth. "It was just—"

"Out of left field."

"Yeah. So what prompted you to do that?" Eli watched Chase's face fall. Seriousness settled in. Whatever it was, it was enough to turn his light-hearted friend into a solemn statue.

"That's not all the news. I'm moving to New York."

The announcement hit Eli like a load of cinder blocks being thrust at him. It was a lot to take in, and he was struggling. His best friend, in a week, had completely unraveled his own life. "But—why?" Those words were the only ones he could push past the barrier in his throat.

"I know it seems sudden, but I've been thinking about it for the past couple of months." Chase pulled in front of Eli's house and switched off the ignition, looking down at the keys in his hand. "You know

I've been active with Georgia Equality, helping them to get a good foothold here in Atlanta for the last few years."

"And you've been rocking the hell out of it," Eli mused proudly.

"They've done just that and are opening another chapter in Savannah."

"Okay, but how does this translate to you moving to New York?"

"There is this other factor in the mix of things. You know the ball this past Halloween?" Chase glanced over, seeing Eli nod. "I met someone."

"Who'd you meet? And why is this the first time I'm hearing about this?" Eli asked.

"I had my reasons for keeping it under wraps, and before I tell you who, I want you to know I didn't know about your connection to him at first... It wasn't until several weeks later that I found out. I just, uh, I just really like him," Chase let out the last sentence in a sigh, and moved his hands to the steering wheel again, gripping it like a life preserver. "We connected like I've never connected with anyone before."

"Chase, you have to know. I'm happy for you regardless of who this person is. All I have ever and will ever wish for you is happiness."

Chase looked over at Eli. "William Collins."

"You can't be serious, Chase," Eli blurted out. "He's seventeen years your senior!" Silence filled the air for several minutes. "So, you and William are moving to New York together? Do you love him?"

Chase shook his head and wiped a tear from his cheek. "No, but I could."

"Chase, you can't just drop everything. Give up your whole life for someone you don't love."

"Listen Eli, I know you have this vision of what someone ought to do. The path they should take, and god knows, I know you've got this idealistic view of love. But not everyone is you. Not everyone can afford to take those risks, and I live in a very different world than you do."

"No, you don't! You live in the same world I do!" Anger welled up, warming Eli's face.

"I don't!" Chase shouted back. "You're a straight white man! You can't even imagine what it has been like for me my whole life. To be not only a black man but also gay? It's an impossible field to navigate, especially after the epidemic."

"You've been doing it, though. I've seen you do it!"

"And that's the problem. The looks I get, snide comments, some muttered under their breath and others blatantly told should not be something I have to put up with." Chase wiped his nose with the sleeve of his shirt. "It hurts, Eli. The burden of it all I've carried silently and now I've a chance to be free of it."

Eli slumped back in his seat and hung his head. Everything Chase said stung. Had he really been that blind to how this all affected him? "Why, New York?"

"The mayor of New York City just signed a new law this past July which protects domestic partnerships. It's the closest thing to marriage Will and I can get, and New York City has a robust LGBT community. There is safety there."

Eli nodded. "When do you leave?"

"I wanted to wait till you got back so I could tell you in person. I leave tomorrow."

"Tomorrow?"

"Will has concluded his business in Meryton. He already had a ticket to leave tomorrow. I just bought mine for the same flight and time."

Eli nodded and sat quietly. "I'm going to miss you."

"It won't be long before you're back up in New York for your internship and you can stay with us!"

"This is true. I guess I'm just sad that I was gone for the last week of you being here," Eli said. He pulled on the handle and opened the door before looking back at Chase. "Call me before you leave and when you get there? I just want to know you're safe."

"You got it," Chase said, smiling. "I'll see you soon."

"I love you, bro."

"Ditto."

Eli got out and opened the back door to retrieve his suitcase. Sadness filled him and his jaw clenched to keep his emotions at bay. Deliberate slow steps backwards patted out the beat of his inner turmoil as he waved goodbye. He watched until Chase's car turned off his street before he turned back to the chaos of his home life.

Chapter 22

Heaviness plagued Eli for days after. He tried to push Darci and their exchange out of his mind multiple times but failed miserably. It had been a week since she'd dumped her feelings on him. The last thing he needed if he was being honest. The fact she did it when she did, after having broken up James and Charleigh's relationship, disgusted him.

The end of the New York trip came at a good time. He needed to leave the madness behind, but that was infinitely easier said than done. His whole dynamic was off and there was no Chase around to help bring him back down and sort his thoughts. They were eating him alive. The wear of his sleepless nights played out in front of everyone. James had already asked several times what was wrong. Eli just couldn't be the one to tell him the truth about Charleigh, and Darci's place in all of it. Eli barely left his room to eat.

A light rap on his door drew him out from under his blankets. "Go away," Eli muttered.

"Eli?" A soothing voice cooed through the door.

He turned towards the door and laid there staring at it, unsure if he cared enough to respond. The last thing he wanted was to have his moping impeded upon, and he certainly didn't want to deal with the hassle of entertaining someone with conversation. Why couldn't people just leave him the hell alone?

"Your brother is worried about you. Can I come in?"

Ah, so it was James who'd overstepped and reached out to Gianna. He didn't have the emotional or mental fortitude to handle any of Darci's and her bullshit. "What do you want?"

"Just to talk to you and see if you're okay."

"I'm fine."

"Well, can you at least let me in so we can talk?"

Eli sighed, kicked off his covers, and got up to open the door. He left it hanging open and walked back to his bed and flopped down.

"Hello to you too."

"Listen, I'm not in a talkative mood, Gia."

"I can see that," she said, crossing her arms and pressing them to her chest, leaning against the door frame. "What caused this downward spiral?"

"I'd rather not talk about it."

"From what I've heard, you made rather the impression on Keats."

"You've heard? What exactly have you heard, Gia?"

"Well," she said, uncrossing her arms and pushing herself off the door opening. "For starters, you brought your Southern charm to the company via unfiltered comments."

"Look, not that I want to get into it, but my eyes were opened about the person Darci is. Don't even get me started on that twat Gavin and his bastard boss, Keats." Eli threw his hands in the air dismissively.

"Ah, so that's what has your axle bent," Gia said, moving to sit on the edge of his bed. "I know them well enough, and they are some of the most miserable people I've ever met in my life."

"Miserable is an understatement," Eli sighed, running his hand over his face, and sat up. "My desk is in front of Darci's office partition wall. Should be easy enough to overhear conversations, and apparently I'll be Darci's servant. Which means I have access to all her appointments, plans, meetings, etcetera."

"Oh, that puts you in a prime position, then."

"Yeah, it does. I normally wouldn't relish taking a company down, but after my personal experience, I'll lose no sleep over this."

"When do you go back to stay the semester?"

"I'll finish up this semester, which is about a month left, and then head back up there after Christmas. I'll be there through May."

"Eli, you don't have to do this."

"It is less about you, and more about moral and ethical principles." Eli laid back down and covered up. "And now, I'd like to go back to sleep, if you don't mind."

Gia nodded. "You take care of yourself, okay, Eli?"

Eli raised his hand and waved her off, waiting for the click of the latch bolt before throwing the covers back off himself. There was no peace to be had at home, either. He went to his dresser and took out his favorite cotton long sleeve shirt, pulling it over his head. Space and time to think while being left alone were vital. The room felt stuffy, making it hard for him to breathe.

He opened the window, sliding out onto the rooftop, unsure of where to go. This was the shitty part of living in a small town. No matter where you went, someone who knew you would see you and come up wanting to talk. Maybe he'd just stick to the woods and be alone with the creaking trees and scurrying sounds of animals. Yes, that's what his soul needed—the faux sense of freedom.

The house was dark and quiet when he got back from his hours-long trek in the woods. It'd been a good call. Eli felt refreshed and had figured out his next steps. There was a slight spring in his footfall as he walked up the stairs to his room. The ever present weight pinning him down finally seemed to be letting up.

He flipped the light on in his room and saw an envelope and a note on his bed. "Fantastic," Eli said as he walked over to his bed and picked up the note.

This came for you while you were gone. Figured I'd leave it here for you to see. Mom went all arm flail mode about you not being back for the Christmas tree lighting ceremony at the town square. Something about family tradition, been doing it since we were young boys, etc. You know how she gets, so prepare yourself for the ear full that is probably going to be leveled at you when we get back home.

James

Eli discarded the note and picked up the envelope. There was no return address listed, just his name and home address. Postage marked it as from New York. He threw the letter back on the bed, having half a mind to just burn it. What more could anyone from that hellish place have to say to him? Reluctantly, Eli picked it back up and flipped it over, opening it. Inside were thin and neatly folded, smooth sheets of paper, and only god knew the contents scribbled on them.

Chapter 23

E^{li,}

Please know that this letter isn't an attempt to convince you to rethink your stance on my apparent, disgusting affection towards you, nor is it an effort to apologize for my observations regarding what happened between us as I believe I'm right in making them. What I can't allow is the slight made against my reputation and ultimately character. There are two significant charges you laid upon me last we spoke. One being the dissolution of your brother and my friend's relationship, the other, gross wrongs done to someone whom our family took in and treated as our own blood.

I don't have any intention of levying any more pain your way, as I think we've adequately harmed each other. All I ask is that you read the explanations for my actions because, believe it or not, I have my reasons. I know I have no right to ask this, but I hope you'll pardon my openness and honesty regarding both these matters.

Charleigh, being my best friend, is one to fall in love quickly. Her experience with your brother wasn't unlike anything I'd seen before. I've had to take great pains in helping to save her from her impulses. Many of which, had I not, would have destroyed her. Either via irreparable damage done to her reputation or rendered her a pariah of her family and society. Your brother was no different to me than all these other interests. I saw her immediate attachment to your brother as troubling. It's validated by others who attended the Netherfield party of the observed attachment they both had for one another.

It was at the Masquerade Ball after I'd had the honor of sharing a dance with you, that I realized Charleigh was being played because of her wealth and status by your family after overhearing your mother blather about how the relationship would be a great asset for your family's social standing. This spurred me into action. I watched Charleigh's behavior and realized that she was invested in James like I'd never witnessed before. I also observed James. He was attentive and open, but none of these things spoke of the wish for deeper involvement. I deduced that because of the lack of reciprocation, it would be best to remove her from the situation, saving her from further heartache.

If what you've said about your brother's feelings towards Charleigh is true, which I can only suspect considering your knowledge of your brother's inner thoughts and feelings, then I have been misguided. For this error, I have earned your resentment and ire. What I perceived caused significant pain. And while we could still argue your lack of connections as it pertains to me, it isn't something I bind Charleigh to. Her duties aren't as great as my own and thus she's not held to such high standards. I want to note that you and James carried yourselves respectably. I can only find the likes of which honorable.

This brings me to the part I played in this. Karl was equally worried about Charleigh and sought my help. As Charleigh has long considered my advice to be sound and in her best interest, convincing her of your brother's disregard was, sadly, easily done. I explained how absurd it would be to bring someone of your brother's stature into the family and that she had deceived herself in her reading of James' emotions. I've nothing else to say or explain regarding this matter. What's done is done and I've no other apologies. If I hurt your brother's feelings, I did not knowingly do it, and I've yet to find my feelings on this condemnable.

As for Ms. Wickham, I can feel righteous in my behaviors and actions to her. You've been told falsities regarding the slight against her. The only way for me to explain its entirety is to explain the whole of her connection to my family. Her father was a respectable man who worked for my father. His management of Pemberley estates was impeccable and so it isn't a far stretch to think my father would return the faithful service with his own expression of high regard. This came about after her parents passed away. My father took her in and cared for her as his own. He felt it was his duty to honor the memory of her father to see his daughter thrive and be successful. Gianna had never wanted for anything and had the finest education made available to her. We put her through college at Harvard University and she was to gain a place within De Bourgh Publishing as an editor, which is aligned with my father's wishes. I, being the executor of his will, would know. This, coupled with various debaucheries while at college, led to my questioning of my father's judgment, though I kept my observations to myself.

After returning from college, Gianna continued to use her living stipend for illicit drugs and gambling. This prohibited her from being able to perform at her job as one of the top editors to the company and thus garnered her forced resignation. It was with her reputation in mind, which she'd given no thought to protect, that I paid her a year's severance and attended to all her debts she'd racked up. It was after shoring up her debts that I learned she sought to marry my brother George. I've no *doubt in it being an effort to continue to siphon money from my father's estate. Beyond that, my brother was very much her junior and not at all old enough to understand the implications of his or her actions. I know part of her wanting to attach herself to my brother was in sheer malice towards me, as she felt like I'd wronged her in the removal of her position within the company. Had this been allowed, her revenge on me would have been complete since George is under my care until he turns twenty-one.*

All of this is an honest retelling of the events surrounding Gianna Wickham. I trust you're now able to understand my ire regarding Ms. Wickham and you'll grant some leniency for my behaviors towards her. As you've become acquainted with Kate, she can verify all of this, as she is intimately aware of all the transgressions, and was also an executor of my father's will and is privy to all the information I'm relaying to you. This should ease you from having to take only my word as absolute truth.

You may wonder why I'd not mentioned this during our conversation and I'll admit, it hurt my pride. I couldn't think clearly in order to facilitate a rebuttal to the charges you laid at my feet. It took me aback hearing the sheer inaccuracies no doubt told to you by Gianna. I have nothing left to say outside; I wish you nothing but the best.

Respectfully,
Darci

Eli sat on his bed and stared at the wall, allowing her words to fully sink in. He looked back down at the pages in his hand. Her meddling in his brother's affairs was to be expected, though now to see it from her perspective and knowing what his mother said caused his face to flush with shame. How was Darci to know James' feelings towards Charleigh or about his natural shyness with public displays of affection?

What blind-sided him were Gianna's truths that she'd harbored from him, letting him believe she was wholly wronged, when that couldn't be further from the reality of it all. She'd made a fool of him, as had his family. A seething rage filled him. He'd been wrong about Darci because of lies and the judgment of others. He couldn't possibly show his face in New York after all of this, but he had to.

Chapter 24

T he last few weeks were painful. Eli was still nowhere close to figuring out how to deal with the information given to him. James could tell something plagued him, but stopped poking after Eli'd griped at him for mentioning Gianna's name. He felt like a rubber band that was about to snap—pushed to his limits. His whole life had been in upheaval since Charleigh rented out Netherfield Park last August. Four months of near constant barrage of drama was taking its toll.

"You almost finished packing?"

"Almost."

"Eli, before you go away for months, can you tell me what is bothering you?"

Eli paused, folding his shirt, throwing it into the suitcase. "Maybe talking with someone about this instead of trying to shoulder it by myself would be good. Considering, I'm about to spend the next four months working with someone—"

"Who is a miserable excuse for a human being?"

"Someone I'm afraid I've misjudged."

"How have you misjudged her? I've seen the way she's behaved. And you told me how she and her family treated Gianna."

"Apparently, Gianna has been twisting the truths to play to her narrative. And knowing her history, I'm fairly certain I was being used to gather information on Darci and De Bourgh Publishing."

"Are you sure Darci is trustworthy?"

"I'm pretty sure, especially since she has another person who can verify the claims made in her letter." Eli slumped down on his bed. "I don't know how to face Darci again and I really don't know how to handle this Gianna thing. Do I confront her?"

James moved to sit next to Eli, putting his arm around his shoulder. "This is what's been weighing on you and making you a nightmare to live with?"

"Yeah."

"Why didn't you tell me sooner instead of suffering in silence?"

Eli hung his head, knowing full well why he'd avoided telling James anything about the letter. It hurt more than his pride. The realization of why Darci had come between James and Charleigh was just as lofty. He knew that part of the letter would have to remain his burden to carry alone. "I didn't want to gossip."

"You, gossip?" James chuckled. "That is one thing you never do, namely because you put a quick stop to it with the tip of your tongue, cutting those down with your snark." James got up from the bed, his demeanor morphing from jovial to anger as he paced back and forth. "To think our family has been accepting of Gianna the whole time you were away in New York. She came by the house almost every day just to hang out."

"It's not like any of you knew who she really was."

"No, but it's upsetting. She painted herself as being alone in the world. We took her in." James stopped pacing, looking at Eli. "We invited her along to see the tree lighting ceremony. She used us too, Eli."

"I know."

"And you knew about this the entire time she was here for Christmas! No wonder you were distant to her. I thought you were just being an asshole for no reason."

"To be fair, from the outside, I can understand your assumption. So what do I do? Do I confront her?"

"Honestly," James sighed, "I think we should just let it stay between us for now. No sense in causing loads of drama. I'll just imply that you two had a falling out, and that is why Gianna is no longer welcome around here."

"Do you think that will work?"

"Well, it certainly seemed that there might have been something between you two since she arrived in town. We all had thought that you both were an item already and just said nothing to us about it. So, yeah, I think playing it that way will work."

Eli nodded, grabbing his unfolded shirt and stood up. "Are you taking me to the airport?"

"You know how upset mom is that you're leaving and dad has to work. I dropped dad off at the shop and took the day off just to take you."

"I'm going to miss you, James."

"Oh, don't you say goodbye. You'll be back soon."

Eli watched the trees passing by. The trip to the airport felt different. Last time was filled with anxiety and dread. This time, it was solemn. He knew that when he made it to Chase's apartment, he could have a full on breakdown. One that he desperately needed.

James pulled up to the terminal, put the car in park, and looked at Eli. His eyes filled with worry. "You're gonna be okay."

Eli unbuckled his seatbelt and sat staring out the window for a moment before nodding. "You have Chase's number?"

"Yeah, I put it on the fridge, so if anyone needs to get a hold of you, they can."

Without looking over at James, Eli pulled the handle of the door and slid out, shutting the door. James popped the trunk so Eli could get his suitcase and duffle bag. He watched Eli close the trunk lid and stride through the sliding glass doors. There was no goodbye, but James knew Eli's heart.

"He'll be okay," James said to himself as he pulled away. "He's always okay."

"You goin' my way, handsome?"

Eli brought his hand up to shield his eyes from the sun, peering in the direction the familiar voice came from. Chase was leaning against a taxi, arms folded, a wide smile on his face. He felt the heaviness lift away the closer he got to his best friend. Eli dropped all his gear and wrapped his arms around Chase, squeezing him while attempting to keep from crying. It caught Chase off guard, but he wrapped Eli in a hug and held him there, letting his best friend fall apart.

"You okay?"

"Chase, I'm anything but okay. I miss having you around."

"Boy, you know I'm just a phone call away, right?" Chase said, pulling away to look Eli in the face.

"Yeah, but phone calls aren't the same thing as you being there in person."

"Well, lucky you, you'll have me in flesh and blood for a few months," Chase said while bending down to pick up Eli's suitcase and bag. "Let's get out of here."

Eli opened the back passenger door and slid into the seat, waiting for Chase to put his luggage in the trunk and join him. The taxi driver's head was bobbing along to music while patiently waiting for Chase to get in. When Chase climbed in and shut the door, the driver clicked the meter and pulled away.

"So, you gonna fill me in on what's been happening since I've been away?"

"Oh, we'll get into it later, I'm sure, but honestly, I'm tired of talking and thinking about it," Eli said, his focus on his clasped hands. "How have things been here for you?"

"They've been good. I've been helping to set up a new chapter here. It's a lot of work and time away from home, but it suits me."

"And William is okay with you being gone most of the day?"

"Will, has his real estate management and I have my activism," Chase chuckled out. "Not to mention, I think if I were holed up with him for even half the day, I'd be driven mad."

Eli shook his head. "I still don't see why you two are together. Shouldn't you be with someone you can enjoy your time with? Ya know, don't want to be away from?"

"Our partnership is beneficial. I know you don't see things the way I see them and struggle to understand it, Eli."

"I guess if you're happy and all," Eli said.

"I am. Oh," Chase exclaimed. "I forgot to tell you. Tomorrow, we have a visit with Will's patron."

"Patron?"

"You know how he is in the real estate business?"

"How could I forget, considering William is keen on reminding my father that once he dies, he is taking the house back," Eli said bitterly.

"I know there's tension between you two—"

"That's an understatement."

"Anyway, Will has an investor. He scopes out properties that are an excellent investment and buys them for his patron. His investor allows him to manage them for pretty good pay."

"Does this investor have a name?"

"Yes," Chase said, falling silent and not volunteering any more information.

"Who is it, Chase?" Eli prayed that the name Darci didn't fall from his lips.

"Keats De Bourgh."

Eli sat back in the seat, wishing to just fade away. Darci would have been better than Keats. And to have a visit scheduled tomorrow, Eli was ready to have the driver turn the car around. "I'm not going tomorrow."

"You have to."

"I don't have to do anything," Eli said, crossing his arms across his chest.

"Keats is already expecting you."

"Chase, I already told you on the phone how much I detest that man. Why would you blab about me coming to visit early? I have two weeks before I need to see his face."

"You can thank Will. When he heard you were interning with De Bourgh Publishing, he, of course, had to name drop you."

"Of course he had to," Eli quipped, rolling his eyes.

"Ellington Bennet," Chase chided. "Put on your big boy pants."

"Fine. I'll go—for you."

The rest of the car ride to Chase's apartment was silent. A smashing first day back in the hellscape that'd be his life for the next several months.

Chapter 25

Rosings Park grounds looked stark in the daylight of dead winter. The ambience of the lit drive was nowhere to be found. Twisted and jagged branches of once beautiful full trees lined the way, painting a chilling picture. Its foreboding presence did little to calm Eli's nerves. He was sure that Keats wore a facade to impress those at the party while introducing him to guests. Heaven knew what was waiting for him now.

"Isn't it one of the most grand estates in all of New York, dare I say, the world!" William exclaimed as they began walking up the drive. "Truly a remarkable gem from the Gilded Age and the fact that you are working for Mr. De Bourgh is, in its own right, a grand feat."

Eli looked over at Chase to see his friend just smiling and nodding at William's prattling. He set his jaw in determination. For Chase, he'd suffer and play nice. "I'm fortunate, indeed."

"Please, when you go back home, let your father know the company you've found yourself in. I'm sure it will give him something to be immensely proud of you for."

Pressure built up inside Eli. His eyes narrowed. "I will."

"I wonder if what you've been doing with your life so far has garnered such acclaim and respect."

Chase glanced at Eli's face, sensing the brewing anger that dwelled just below the surface. "Will, after we visit for a bit, I'll take Eli on a tour of the gardens while you and Keats settle business affairs."

"That's a great idea! There isn't a prettier view or parcel of land in all the nation, if not the world."

"So you've said," Eli retorted, pursing his lips and moving behind Chase while William rapped on the door. The same elderly gentleman came to the door and opened it. "Good morning, Mr. Collins and Mr. Lucas."

"Morning, Marlon. We're here with a guest, Mr. Eli Bennet."

Marlon looked over at Eli and nodded. "I recognize him from the festivities last month. Good morning to you as well. Please come in and I'll fetch Mr. De Bourgh for you." He held open the door, allowing all three visitors in before shutting it behind them and scurrying off to find his employer.

"Keats is the most generous of hosts and patrons. You'll go far in this life now that you have his support." William said.

"I'm sure I will."

Echos of hollow footsteps announced the coming presence of the manor's owner. Keats donned tan slacks and a maroon polo shirt, his hair left unstyled, making him look approachable and real. A pair of dark tan boat shoes finished his casual look, leaving Eli unsettled.

"Good morning, William," Keats said, smiling. He gave a friendly nod in Chase's direction before his face hardened and his eyes narrowed. "Mr. Bennet. Have you all had breakfast yet?"

"We picked something up on the way, as we wouldn't dream of being a burden to you."

"If you kiss his butt any harder, you'll find your lips wedged some-where between Keats' larynx and trachea," Eli whispered under his breath, garnering a heated glare from Chase, who'd heard just enough to understand what he'd said.

"I'm sorry? What was that, Eli?" Keats inquired.

"Nothing, sir. I was just going over my checklist of things to do before I start at De Bourgh." A curt nod was all that Keats gave in response.

"Do you mind if I take Eli out to tour the grounds while you and Will talk business?"

"Not at all, Chase," Keats said with a half-hearted smile.

The expansive property, under normal circumstances, would have taken his breath away. Acres of garden accentuated the pond, harken-ing back to an era of exquisite poshness. Rose bushes lined the walk-way, fostering a curiosity in Eli about the colors of their blooms. Chase and Eli meandered the path in a comfortable silence.

"Are we ever going to talk about the elephant?"

"Which elephant?" Eli asked. He knew this was bound to come up at some point, though he'd hoped it wouldn't. Just thinking about everything was a level of exhaustion he didn't care to take on.

"Well, I assume there is one by the name of Darci, another named Gianna, and then you've got Keats." Chase shrugged and stuck his hands in his pockets. "I guess I should correct myself and say *elephants.*"

Eli glanced over at Chase, folding his arms across his chest. "Gianna is a liar. Darci is insufferable still. And Keats is a pretentious twat. That about sums it all up."

"I guess." Chase stopped walking, turning to Eli. "From what I gather, these last couple of months have been difficult for you. Lord knows what I've missed, but you're going to have to figure out a way to deal with," Chase waved his hand up and down, "all of this, whatever this is."

"You don't think I know that!" Eli huffed out, turning to be toe to toe with Chase. "I've not had a moment's peace, away from anyone tied to those three people, in order to process. More shit is just shoveled on top of more shit." His arms fell to his side, hands balling into fists. He shook his head and walked off, leaving Chase behind.

It'd been years since he snapped at Chase like that. All he could see in that moment was red, and he knew the consequences if he didn't remove himself immediately. Of all the things swirling around in his mind, one kept forcing its way to the surface.

How foolish he'd been to fall captive to a conniving snake. He hated himself for it. It wasn't just his ego that lay in tatters, but his moral compass. Gianna had preyed upon him—taken advantage of him—and he couldn't retaliate. The evilness would remain buried, never to see the light of day. This world would go on thinking highly of a twisted individual who cared not for anyone other than herself. Reconciling all of that was the ultimate struggle, and one he wasn't sure he'd be capable of. At the moment, there was only one course of action that would sate him—a lit match tossed on a kerosene drenched pile and watching the world burn.

Chapter 26

H is misery grew as time went on. Eli skirted around talking about his feelings for the past three months. It was only a matter of time before he'd have to talk about them, though in the meantime he was quite content in keeping to himself. He spent his days outside of Chase and Will's apartment, wandering the city aimlessly and taking in the sights. There'd been some nice finds, like hidden antique shops, but his favorite was a hole in the wall book store run by an older couple.

They had no children, which suited them, as they littered their store with photos of them both in foreign and exotic places. Their travels culminated in this shop. Everywhere they went, they'd purchase books to bring back, many of which were rare copies. The stories intrigued Eli, and he'd sit and listen to them ramble on and on. Every so often, the woman would touch her husband's hand and gently correct his version of events, which made Eli grin. This was what he wanted out of life, and meeting them only solidified this. The soft ring of the bell announced his arrival. Eli strode in, peeled off his jacket, and placed it over the chair closest to the door. It'd become his spot.

"Eli! How are you this morning?"

"I'm great, Mrs. Abrams."

"How many times do I have to tell you to call me Esther," she said, walking over, wrapping him in a hug. "You'll have to forgive Frank. He isn't feeling well and stayed home today."

"Is he okay?"

Aged lines ran deeper on her forehead. "We received some rather hard news late yesterday about the tests that the doctors ran on him."

Eli's stomach fell. "Do you mind if I ask what tests?"

"It was something I'd been worried about that only seemed to solidify when you came into our lives." Esther hugged her arms around her chest, seeking comfort and support from within. "I know you've undoubtedly noticed my gentle corrections of the stories Frank joyously shares with you. He didn't struggle like this until recently, and it's getting worse."

Her pause said everything he needed to know. Eli wanted to rescue her from saying the words. "Alzheimer's or dementia?"

Esther's head bobbed slowly up and down. "Rapid onset dementia."

Eli ran his hands through his hair and shook his head, unwilling to accept that Frank would be no-more-than a hollowed-out shell of what he once was. The love they had for one another was a candle flickering until ultimately the light would finally burn out.

"What will you do, Esther?"

She smiled warmly at Eli. "We shall go on living our lives together for as long as we can. I've chosen to close the store because I don't want to waste one moment with Frank." Tears streamed down her face. "We'll go on our grandest adventure yet. Where to? I don't know, but it will be us together, hand in hand, until the end."

It was Eli's turn to wrap her in a hug. "I wish you both nothing but the best. Thank you for taking my aimless soul in and sharing your lives with me."

"Eli, can I give you a bit of advice?"

"Mhmm."

"Whatever has your soul in such a state of unrest, handle it. Life's too short and you're bound to miss all the beauty it has for you if you keep on the road you're on."

Eli gave Esther a squeeze, nodding in agreement. "I will. You guys take care and if you travel to far-off places, send me a postcard or two."

Esther stepped back and watched Eli reclaim his jacket, sliding it on. "I will," she said, her eyes gleaming with tears, as she watched Eli open the door and look back for the last time.

The walk back to the apartment was somber. Overcast drizzle that fell from the heavens mirrored his mood. Eli knew Esther was right about getting things sorted, and to do that he needed to make amends, regardless of Darci's behaviors previously, she shared her heart, something he could respect. Her being open also saved him from any further entanglements with Gianna.

Eli turned the knob, opening the front door. Chase sat on the couch and looked up, eyes honing in on Eli. "Chase, I'm sorry," Eli said, while closing the door behind him. "I know I've been unbearable the last few months and my behavior towards you wasn't justified."

Chase scooted over on the couch and patted the seat next to him. "I know. I've been patiently waiting for you to come to your senses. And I'm glad you did because I need you to do me a favor."

Eli walked over to the couch and flopped down next to Chase. "I've made such a big mess of things and I feel like an idiot. You're my best friend," Eli said, dejected. "What's the favor?"

"You think you can cover down on Best Man duties for me?"

Eli's eyes widened, and his jaw dropped. "Chase!"

"I know, I know. It's not a pairing you approve of," Chase muttered.

"Chase, I'm not remotely qualified to give my thoughts." Eli let out a deep belly laugh. "I mean, have you seen the shitfest that is my life? When do you need my services?"

"Oh, it won't be for at least another year. We're looking for a place big enough for us to build a life together," Chase said, looking around the apartment. "This one bedroom and barely enough room to sit on the toilet and not shut yourself in the bathroom door business isn't for me. And I hate that you have had to sleep on the couch because I don't have space for a guest room."

"Chase, you know better than anyone that I can sleep anywhere. Look at the chaos I was raised in."

"Fair. Okay, now back to you and your shitfest of a life. What big mess are you talking about?"

"Outside of my being an ass to you? From the moment that Darci came into my life, I've set to judging her."

"To be fair, she's done the same thing to you."

"I know, but I shouldn't have let my pride nor prejudice take the driver's wheel, even if she's allowed hers to."

"So, where does this leave you?"

"Well," Eli sighed, "I suppose I'll reach out and apologize. It's all I can do, honestly. The ball will be in her court after that."

Chase patted his hand on Eli's knee. "I think that is rather mature of you, Eli. Can I ask what gave you this kick in the ass?"

"About a month and a half ago, I found this small bookstore and met a sweet woman, Esther. Her husband, Frank, was just diagnosed with dementia, " Eli said. "It was hard news to hear. Her parting words sucker punched me and made me realize I needed to set things right with people in my life."

"Good," Chase said, standing up and walking towards his bedroom. "I'll let you get to it then," he shouted back at Eli before shutting the door.

Eli got up and strode to the corded phone attached to the wall. He reached into his back pocket, pulled out his wallet and thumbed through the contents until he located Darci's business card which had her home phone number scrawled on the back, and removed it from its home. The hard plastic was cold to touch as he took it off the receiver and pushed buttons. Knuckles of his hand that clutched the phone were white. Nervousness stacked on top of itself with every unanswered ring. He'd give it a few rings before he hung up and there was no way he was leaving a message on her answering machine if it picked up instead. What should he say? Should he make small talk or go straight to the point? What if she–

"Hello?"

At that moment, he wished she wouldn't have answered. "Darci?"

"Eli?"

"Yeah."

"Do you need something for the High Hopes project?"

"Uh, no. I, um, well—" Eli let out a sigh. "I'd like to discuss your letter."

"Oh." Darci's tone sank a bit.

"Listen, I'd like to meet up and talk about things, if that is okay with you."

"When were you thinking?"

"I left my calendar with your appointments at the office. Can I get back to you on Monday and set something up, then?"

"Pemberley isn't too far away from the city. Do you maybe just want to come over here tomorrow?" Darci's voice had shifted from a low morose tone to a more upbeat one. "I can make dinner and you can meet George."

"That sounds great."

"The local historical society has a tour scheduled for tomorrow, so I'll be away for a portion of the day."

"What time should I plan to be there?"

"Let's say six. Does that work for you?"

"It does. I'll see you then, Darci."

"Okay. Bye, Eli."

His chest burned from the breath he'd been holding. He hung the receiver back on the hook. *A historical society*. A smirk swept across Eli's face as he reached over the counter to grab the phone book, thumbing through the yellow pages to find any historical associations. He'd nothing planned for tomorrow, especially now, seeing as though his favorite perch had closed for good.

Chapter 27

Incessant chatter from curious tourists filled the air around Eli. Many had come to the big city for their spring break vacation as was clear by their fanny packs and consistent flashes of light from the disposable cameras that'd inevitably capture more of their fingers than the actual subjects they'd aimed to photograph. Eli watched the countryside pass frame by frame in his window. He was glad they'd room on the bus for his late registration. The times lined up well. They would spend three hours on the grounds, lunch included, and have an hour back to the bus depot. He'd be back home by four, which would give him time to shower and get ready to go back this evening.

Sounds of awe stirred him to focus his attention on where everyone looked. The forest area opened up to a rolling hill landscape, pruned and preened to perfection. The estate was ten times more beautiful than Rosings Park, even if it was smaller. White colonial pillars stood out in stark contrast to the red brick. Large windows framed by dark blue painted shutters loomed over barren flower boxes. Each side of the house's gables had a balconied inlet lined with decorative white wrought iron balusters and railing. Trimmed hedges and swirled juniper topiaries surrounded a modest two tiered fountain.

Pemberley lacked the cold and impersonal rigidity of Rosings. This was obviously a beloved home and not a beacon of flaunted money. Eli's shoulders relaxed as he sat back, waiting for the bus to come to a stop and the hoards of people to file off. He'd be damned if he'd be in the thick of things and getting trampled. Once the last person had filed off the bus, Eli moved down the aisle, planting his first steps into Darci's world. Guilt and shame for the assumptions he'd made about her welled to the surface. How wrong he'd been.

The crowd moseyed around the gravel drive, taking in the towering two-storey with their mouths hanging open. A young woman opened the door, her hair pulled up into a loose bun on top of her head, red wisps sprouting off every which way. Her relaxed nature was inviting. She wore a long colorful sweater with black leggings and high-top sneakers.

"Welcome to Pemberley. I'm Haley, and I'll be your guide today," she said, greeting the masses with a wide smile. "If you'll follow me, we'll get the tour started so we can keep to the schedule and make sure we hit the half-way point by lunchtime." Haley turned around and walked off, waving her hand, signaling for everyone to follow.

Cream wainscoted walls with three-step crown molding carried through several feet to a large opening. Antique brass sconces lined both sides of the hallway, unlit. Footsteps echoed with each step on the black-and-white checkered patterned floor. Off white scrolled pillars at the end of the hallway opened up to a towering ceiling. An elegant glass chandelier hung above; the light filtered through crystal shards and danced high on the wall. On either side of the room were stairs lined with wrought-iron railing, the middle area continuing further back, highlighting a wall of windows.

Eli trailed behind the group, filling into the open room. His eyes scanned the walls, taking in the large golden frames that delicately decorated them. The oil paintings ranged from floral and fruit stills to renaissance depictions of lovers, angels, and battles fought. As he meandered through, paying no attention to what Haley was saying, he moved through open French doors to the room on the left of the opening. Ribboned beige wallpaper with small floral detail lined the upper half of the walls, as wainscoting accented the bottom half of the wall. To his right was a sitting area furnished with two deep mahogany armchairs and a loveseat. The upholstery of the loveseat and two chairs were Pelham blue, contrasting with the beauty of the arms and clawed feet of each piece. Flames crackled in the ornate fireplace, adding to the room's ambience.

Another oil painting hung above the fireplace, this time of an older man, his oldest child standing behind him with her hand on his shoulder, and a young boy who stood next to him on the other side. The man's eyes shone a kindness that he'd seen momentary glimpses of in his daughter. Eli thought back to Darci, caring for his hand. How had he missed the flicker of tenderness in that moment? Oh, right, he was hell-bent on not seeing it. Dark curls fell loosely around Darci's shoulder, a small grin visible to those who knew how to see it. He trained his eyes on the young boy, dressed in suspenders and dress slacks, with a white button-up shirt and a small gold bow tie. The light pouring from the boy's face spoke of sincere joy.

There was a piece missing from the portrait, their mother. How Darci must have felt, taking care of her father and her brother in her mother's stead. Heaviness wadded up in his stomach. Her shoulders had always held the weight of the world.

Eli shook his head and turned to rejoin the group, but they'd moved on. He walked down the hallway under the stairs, hoping they'd gone that way. It opened up to another room with doors at the end of each side. Oversized windows that lined the outer wall beckoned him. He took in the view. Cement stairs led down to a hedge row path that was in slow transition from winter to spring with leaf and flower buds forming. It separated the sidewalk from an outdoor pool with a tiered fountain for the hot tub water to cycle out. Closed umbrellas and sun chairs sparsely lined the poolside, with nannyberry bushes creating a hidden refuge. Further in the distance, he saw a walking path that led to the ocean-side.

He strained to hear any sound from the obnoxious group he'd come with. Quiet ticks of a clock were his only friend. He'd seen enough of the inside. It wasn't museum quality like Rosings Park, and while Pemberley was toned down, it still wasn't homey, like he was used to. It felt impersonal, like a family lived here but only during vacations.

Eli glanced through the window to his left, following the balcony, hoping to find a door to exit onto it. "Bingo," he whispered. The beige painted sturdy oak door opened with ease. Dark paneling was a deep contrast to the brightness he'd just come from. No lights were on in this room and it seemed an off limits portion of the tour, which only furthered his curiosity. It was a great deal smaller and a more intimate room than any he'd seen. An old, cracking leather-backed chair sat behind a moderately sized cherry wood desk.

Time made its presence known in the layer of dust that had accumulated on the flat surfaces. He'd stumbled on a painful secret buried in the recesses of exquisite splendor. Eli glanced around, his heart sinking into the dark abyss of grief. He strode to the backdoor, opening it wide enough to slip through, shutting the door behind him and pressed his forehead against the cool glass. Melancholy prickled him. He let loose a sigh and turned his attention to the staircase. Urgency pecked away, turning his walk into a full sprint.

He ran down the pathways, chest tight and burning. No matter how hard he tried to regulate his breathing, his brain had other plans. The cliff's edge came into view. He slowed, stopping a few yards away, bending over, and placed his hands on his knees. After a minute of resting, Eli straightened and walked to the end of the grassy earth. His breath hitched at the sight of a woman walking the water line. Her long sleeve, white cotton dress, Merino wool shawl, and loose brunette locks fluttered in the sea breeze. He watched her stop occasionally to bend over and pick up an item. She would turn it over in her hand a couple of times before she discarded it. He couldn't take his eyes off her.

Eli watched, mesmerized, as she would skip back to avoid a powerful wave from soaking her. The young girl allowed out of her cage, roamed free. Darci squatted down and rested one arm on her knees while the other set to digging in the wet sand. His heart begged him to traverse the cliff-side path and join her. It took all his will-power to fight the urge. He'd not intrude on her moment of peace.

Darci let out a surprised scream and then a laugh as a wave caught her off guard and drenched her. Eli turned away—contentment filled him. He looked at the clear blue sky, focusing on the puffs of fluffy white clouds, and soaked up the warmth from the sun. His heart felt lighter, and he was genuinely happy. Maybe all he needed to do was allow the darkness of the last several months to melt away and find his inner version of the same type of peace Darci had unlocked. Today, he would take his first step on the path of least resistance.

Chapter 28

Darci focused on the figure's back and watched as he walked out of view. "Eli," she whispered to herself. She turned to retrieve her shoes from the large rock she'd placed them on and ran barefoot up the path. She reached the top of the cliff side and saw Eli looking up at the sky a small distance away. His shoulders had lost their rigidity, and the long held tension that seemed to plague him was nonexistent.

A shiver ran down the base of her spine as she drank him in. His contentment—intoxicating. It'd been a long time since anything left her speechless. Everything in her willed her to go to him. However, uncertainty held her back. What would she say or do? Vulnerability never was her strong suit, and it'd only be a matter of time before he realized her imposition. Darci knew she needed to break the chains that bound her in place, and quickly.

"Good morning, Eli," Darci called out, as she made her way to where he was standing. She was keenly aware her body was visible through the dress that clung to her—highlighting her curves. It did nothing to hide the tones of her skin or the response of her body to him. She employed as much of her shawl as a curtain of protection as she could.

Eli's head snapped around, looking in her direction. His eyes clouded over and shoulders straightened. Great start, Darci. To her surprise, he strode her way, stopping when there was just enough distance between them that sparks of tension were felt. Darci shifted her weight to her other foot while attempting to decode his body language. It was imperative she find her footing before he knocked her off balance. Matters of the heart made it harder for her to find the higher ground. It was all murky and covered in thick fog.

His hands found security in the front pockets of his jeans. "Morning, Darci."

Darci's eyes darted over his face, looking for any sign of openness. Her guard was down, and she hated it. "I postponed my business to next weekend, instead making myself scarce because of the tour."

He freed his right hand from its prison and ran it through his hair, bringing it to rest on the back of his neck. Eli's face flushed with embarrassment. "I'm sorry."

"Sorry? For what?" Darci asked.

"For being here, I guess," Eli said. "I wouldn't have presumed to join the tour if I knew you would be here."

"Oh. Why not?"

Eli crossed his arms in front of his chest and shifted uncomfortably. "This is probably going to sound creepy, though I promise it is the furthest from my intent," he said. "I honestly just wanted to get a better understanding of you before we met this evening."

Darci relaxed at his words. She shivered which reminded her she stood in front of Eli wet, grass riddled, and muddy. "I've got to go," she said with a nod towards the house.

Eli stepped aside, letting her pass by unimpeded. Eyes searing into her back kept her from looking back at him as she walked to the house. There was nothing she could do about covering her backside.

Normally, she enjoyed long hot showers, but this time, the water didn't have enough time to get any warmer than room temperature from start to finish. The joys of antique plumbing. Her routine of hair and skin care products went out the window as she strode to her wardrobe and chose a pair of black leggings and a plain white t-shirt. Darci threw them on and walked to slide her feet into her Keds, grabbing her jean jacket off the post of her bed, slipping into it as she walked out the bedroom door.

She bounded down the stairs and walked to the wall of windows to see if Eli was still out back. Nothing. Darci walked to the front door and opened it, stepping out onto the landing. Her eyes scanned the drive. Eli was halfway to the private road that looped around the property.

Darci ran, kicking up gravel behind her. "Eli," Darci yelled through deep breaths. "Wait!" He stopped and turned. She slowed as she got close to him. "Where are you going?"

"I called a taxi and was going to wait for it on the road."

"Why?"

"Because I shouldn't be here."

"What do you think of the place?"

Eli looked past her and at the house. "I think it's nicer than Rosings." Darci let out a giggle, causing Eli's eyebrows to shoot up. "Sorry, did I say something funny?" The edge in his voice made Darci straighten her face.

"No, no. It wasn't what you said that was funny. It's just my uncle prides himself on his meticulously decorated abode. I've never been able to understand why someone would want their home to feel unlived in." Darci paused and looked back at her house. "Would you like to have an actual guided tour?"

"I don't know. The taxi is already on its way. It might just be best if I leave."

"We can call the company and cancel it, though I don't want you to feel obligated to stay," she said. "I'll respect what you decide." Darci stood teetering on the precipice of the unknown. Anxiety welled up in her as she prepared for the sting of rejection.

Eli looked back at the road and then back at Darci. A moment of breakthrough emotions flitted across his face. "Yeah, okay." He strode over and took his position by her side.

They walked in silence up the driveway to the front door. "What have you seen on the tour so far?" Darci asked, walking through the door to the foyer.

"I can't say I've seen much," Eli admitted while rubbing the back of his neck. "To be honest, I lost the group after wandering into the room over there," he said, pointing to the room he'd traipsed into.

Darci studied his face. He was holding back, though she couldn't figure out what. "Well, let's call the cab company to cancel and we'll start from the top."

Eli walked beside Darci—looking over at her face every so often—enthralled. She was in her element and the most comfortable he'd ever seen her. Her hair fell to her shoulders, wavy and untamed. She looked at him and smiled. Faint freckles he'd never noticed spotted her nose and upper cheeks. The polished and put together facade was nowhere to be seen. He listened intently to the stories of her childhood as they went from room to room. Darci's eyes lit up more and more as she recounted memories of her father. How long had it been since she's been able to share them with anyone?

"George is out right now for his riding lesson. He'll be excited to meet you and will be back before dinner."

Her words broke him of his musings. "I look forward to it."

They'd found their way back to the path they'd been face to face on only a couple of hours before. Comfortable silence filled the air as they walked around, both taking in the beauty of the spring day.

"Eli," Darci said, breaking the silence. "I'd really like it if we could be friends. Can we start over?"

Eli stopped dead in his tracks and looked at her, a cockeyed grin spreading across his face. "I think I'd like that," he replied, holding out his hand. "I'm Ellington Bennet, but you can call me Eli. And you are?"

Darci took his hand and shook it. "I'm Darci Williams. Pleasure to meet you Eli," she said, a radiant smile painted upon her face.

Chapter 29

The warmth of the sun filtering through the bus window added to the serenity of the journey back to the station. Annoying chit-chat had turned into a subdued hum. For the first time in eight months, everything felt right. Unease tangled with excitement over the opportunity to get to know Darci better. Since leaving Pemberley, he could focus on only one thing. Darci. It was odd to him to yearn for more time with her after months of hating her.

"Eli," Chase said as soon as Eli walked through the door. "You need to call your family now." Chase looked at Eli blankly. "Hello? Eli. Earth to Eli," Chase said, waving his hand in front of Eli's face.

"Huh?" Eli'd been so far down the daydream rabbit hole he'd completely missed anything Chase said. "Sorry, Chase. What did you say?"

"I said, you need to call your family. It's important. James wouldn't tell me what was happening, but he sounded upset."

"Shit," Eli said. "Thanks for letting me know," he added, walking to the phone and dialing home.

"Hello?"

"James! What's going on?"

"Eli, it's bad," James said with a sigh.

"Are dad and mom okay?"

"Health-wise, yes. Not sure outside of that. Lance ran off with Gianna."

"What?" Eli couldn't help but shout as shock overtook him.

"It gets worse. Gianna apparently talked him into making a sex tape and now is using it as blackmail."

"Blackmail? What does she even hope to gain from our family? We've nothing to offer her," Eli angrily spat out.

"Your guess is as good as mine. Dad and mom are beside themselves." James sounded tired.

"How long have you guys known about this?"

"Well, the Forster family invited Lance to spend a week at their lake house. Mr. Forster swore he'd monitor him, which was the only reason dad gave him the funds to do it. Thought it would be good for him."

"Fuck."

"Not only is our family reputation on the line but also it will be the last nail in the coffin for the store."

"Wait, what's going on with the store?"

James was silent on the other end for a moment. "It's been struggling to survive for the last few years because of the rapid growth of foreign companies, who can provide services and products for much cheaper. We've been watching other mom and pop shops go under."

"Why did no one tell me this?" Eli leaned against the wall and slid down.

"Because if there was any of us who would make it out of here and do great things we knew it would be you," James cleared his throat. "We knew if we told you that you'd have quit school and sacrificed your future to save the business."

"You're damn right I would have!" Tears welled up in Eli's eyes. "I'm coming home."

"There isn't anything you can even do, Eli. There is nothing any of us can do."

"The fuck there isn't. I can at least be there to help." Eli adjusted the phone cord that was twisting up. "I'm hanging up now and will be on the first flight out I can get. See you soon." He didn't wait to hear James' reply. He stood and hung up before sliding back to the floor.

Eli brought his knees to his chest, resting his crossed arms on them. Just when things seemed to level out for him. He brought his hands up, grabbing fists full of hair and let out a scream. Frustration, anger, and sadness ate him alive.

"Eli? Are you okay?" A worried voice he knew all too well spoke through the front door. "Your wallet fell out of your pocket. Can you let me in?"

He hoisted himself up off the floor. Tears fell as he opened the door, seeing the soft hazel eyes of the new friend he'd made. That was as good as over, too. Eli left the door open and turned away to sit on the couch. Darci walked in, closing the door behind her.

"What's happened?"

Eli punched one of the couch pillows. "Lance and Gianna are what happened."

"Is Lance okay? And what about Gianna?"

"I knew what she was, and I kept silent. James knew a little, but I swore him to secrecy. I could have stopped it, but I didn't."

Darci walked to sit beside Eli. "Explain."

Eli sighed. "Lance ran off with Gianna, and Gianna is blackmailing our family."

Darci got up and paced the room, coming to a stop in front of Eli. "This isn't on you. It's on me. My inaction allowed this to happen."

"Either way. My family's reputation is ruined. I'll leave on the first flight home I can get." Eli stared at his clasped hands. "I can't work for you anymore, either as it could be a media circus that might negatively affect De Bourgh."

Darci nodded. "Can I get you anything or help in some way?"

"Unless, you can magically find both Lance and Gianna, not really."

"Right," Darci said. "I know you've got a lot you need to get done before you leave. I'll leave you to it."

Eli leaned back and closed his eyes after the door closed behind Darci. He would kill Gianna and mildly maim Lance if he got his way for this.

Unfettered rage spewed from Darci as she got into her car. She hated herself for her part in the follies that'd led to this moment. Bile bubbled in her gut. Disgust in herself twisted her face. Gianna might have started it all, but Darci would be the one to finish it. She knew how it would end, even if she had to stoop to the levels of barbaric filth to make Gianna understand. Darci picked up the receiver of her car phone and dialed Kate's number.

"Hello?"

"Kate, I need your help."

"Darci, what's going on?"

"I'm taking Gianna down."

"I didn't think you wanted to do anything else like we'd planned."

"Plans have changed."

"Got it. I'll make the calls."

"Thank you," Darci said, hanging up.

Darci started the car and pulled out of her parking spot. She needed to go to the office and pick a few things up before she headed out of town. If she was going to do this, she'd be going all the way. This would be the last time Gianna would be a problem for anyone.

Chapter 30

E li walked out of the airport and scanned the sparse cars parked, waiting for arrivals. James was supposed to pick him up, but the van was nowhere to be seen. He walked over to a bench and sat down, yawning and stretching. The red-eye flight while quiet was unrestful. His mind kept pouring over the events of the day. It was absurd how in less than a few hours it went from great to terrible.

"Eli."

His aunt's voice was unexpected. Eli stood and grabbed his bag, walking over to her silver sedan. "I thought James was picking me up."

"I offered since James is worn to the bone from working the shop and taking over for your dad at home while he is gone."

"Gone? Where did he go?"

"Mr. Forster communicated that a note Lance left mentioned them running off to Las Vegas. Your dad and Ed have gone to Dallas to see if they stopped there on their way."

"When did you both get into town?"

"Your father called us in the evening the day before yesterday, when word first came from Mr. Forster about Lance having disappeared. Apparently, Lance feigned being sick and stayed back while they went out to eat. When they got back from the restaurant, he was gone."

Eli nodded and got in the car. "And when did they leave?"

"Pretty much as soon as we arrived. We found a flight last night." She paused, looking in her mirrors and pulled out. "It's estimated they got about a fifteen hour head start and it only takes about eleven hours to drive from Atlanta to Dallas. If they stopped along the way, it could be closer to a thirteen or fourteen hour drive."

He pinched the bridge of his nose and let out a defeated sigh. "How the hell are they going to find them in a city that big?"

Silence was his only answer. The rest of the ride home, they shared the oppressive weight of the reality of the situation. Nothing they said would minimize the pain and grief that'd settled on their family like a cloud of gloom. The question lingered in the back of his mind as if there was more at fault than him not exposing Gianna's character. After all, he'd agreed to bring down De Bourgh with Gianna and he'd been radio silent since leaving for New York. A few months ago, this would have surprised him. Now, however, all this did was solidify the testimony given by Darci in her letter.

Overwhelm and exhaustion overtook him. The events of the last several months and recent developments unraveled the threads of his emotional fortitude, pushing him to the edge of his sanity. He was somewhere between just saying fuck it and getting shitfaced and sleeping until it had all passed. It took everything in him to fight the spiraling vortex of depression. His world was spinning wildly out of control and he'd no bearing on what was up or down.

They pulled up in front of the house and parked. Eli stared out the window. Memories of a simpler time played out in front of him.

James and his stick sword fights to the death. A princess saved. Mark's legs dangling out of the tree, his nose buried in a book. Kit and Lance sitting in the flower bed digging in the dirt, pulling out grubs and worms, and making mud pies. How he wished for those days again.

"Eli," Marina said, touching his arm. "Are you okay?"

Eli turned to look at his aunt, placing his hand on hers. "No. No, I'm not."

Marina gave a light squeeze on his arm before removing her hand and taking the keys out of the ignition. "I promise we'll make it through this."

He nodded in silence, exited the car, and walked up the sidewalk to the door. "Keep it together, Eli," he whispered to himself.

The house was asleep. Eli dropped his bag on the floor by the couch and flopped down. It wouldn't be long before chaos ensued, and every moment of peace he could get, he'd treasure.

The putrid stench of thick cigarette smoke made Darci gag. Her eyes burned from each exhaled puff that viciously attacked them. Kate's informant led her to Fat Louis, an underground dive that hosted those who were evading law enforcement. Darci's eyes darted, taking in her surroundings, making note of exits, potentially hostile individuals, all the while mentally preparing herself for what she was about to do. She found a booth in the back corner of the room that faced both entry points and sat down.

Patched vests snaked through the tables, their inhabitants yelling obscenities at each other. A stocky, bald man towards the back of the group made eye contact with Darci. He veered off course, walking her way—a contemptuous smirk danced across his face.

"What do we have here?" he asked, sitting down and sliding his hand from her knee up her thigh. "You looking for a wild ride?"

Darci scooted closer to him, tracing her lips up his neck before stopping at his ear and pausing. "How wild?"

His hands gripped Darci's thigh hard as he turned to face her. "Best railing of your life, wild."

Without missing a beat, Darci grinned. "Can you show me what you'd do starting from here?" she asked, pointing to her navel.

The man's lips curled in lustful want. He pushed the table back so he could slide in between it and her. As he came down, Darci grabbed the edge of his vest and the back of his head, and slammed it on the edge of the table. The sound of the table tipping and falling back on its base mixed with the surprise scream of the man silenced the bar. All eyes were melting into her.

"Get the fuck away from me," Darci hissed out as she scooted away from him.

"Fucking bitch," the man shouted at her, raising his hand to retaliate. His fist came down, aimed squarely at her right cheek, but never made contact.

Darci glared at her saving grace, who still held her aggressors arm back. "Your friend here seems to have a bit of a balance issue," she said with a sardonic grin.

"Rob, here tends to misstep a lot," the younger man retorted. "Come on, Rob. Let's go." He pulled the furious man out of the booth, threw an arm around Rob's shoulders, and trudged off.

She refocused her attention on the doors and looked down at her watch. Fate seemed to be on her side, because when she looked back up, the target sauntered through the front door boisterously laughing as an older man followed close behind. Darci didn't recognize the man, and Lance was nowhere to be seen. She slid out of her booth and approached the couple, who'd stopped at the bar to order drinks.

"Where is Lance?"

Gianna turned around, her face drained of color as she realized who had asked the question. "Ah Darc, how great of you to come visit me in this squalor," Gianna chided.

"I'll not repeat myself."

"The lapping puppy is in the doghouse currently. Sorry," she said, turning back around and picking up conversation with the man again.

Darci grabbed Gianna's shoulder, forcing her to turn back around. "I've got attorneys and reports ready to send to the FBI on your many exploits. You'll release the tape and Lance into my custody or else."

"Or else what, Darci?" Gianna asked with a malicious laugh. "You'll ruin me—again? Been there and done that. You can toss your money around like it makes you special and powerful, but we both know what you are."

"And what am I?"

"A deprived and sad little daddy's girl who is as empty as a drained liquor bottle discarded in the trash. No fun and unwanted."

Radiating pain seared through Darci's hand. Her knuckles throbbed and stung. Gianna's head flung back, the bar catching her and keeping her upright. Darci grabbed the front of Gianna's slinky thigh high dress and pulled her close. "You'll tell me where Lance and the tape are. I can do this all night." Darci reared her arm back to unleash hell upon Gianna if she doubled down.

Gianna wiped the blood from her nose and grinned. "Can it be? Has the prim and proper Darci found someone who broke through that impenetrable exterior?" She looked at the man who stood watching the interaction, completely unbothered by the events. "Come now, Seth, this is a reason to celebrate."

Darci tightened her grip on her dress. "This is the last time I'll ask."

"Oh, Darci. Let's have a drink while I tell you a story of how your precious intern colluded with me to take down De Bourgh. You think he actually cares about you?" Darci's look gave Gianna renewed vigor. She'd hit a nerve. "Oh, that's sweet. You did. Well, no matter. I'm done with Lance, anyway. He's boring, and the tape isn't even that good." Darci let go of Gianna with a shove. "They're both at the motel a couple of blocks over. Number 28. Ta-ta, Darci."

With that information, Darci stepped back and walked out the door. Tears pricked her eyes. She willed Gianna's words to fall off like water on a duck's feathers, to no avail. Gianna found her weakness and weaponized it.

Chapter 31

Days passed with little to no word from either his dad or uncle. Time ticked slowly by. Tension thrived in a normally relaxed chaos. Eli'd taken to helping James at the store, running inventory while his brother handled the clientele. Peopling wasn't Eli's thing. He didn't have the patience or smooth salesperson charisma. Happiness to him was being in the back and never seen.

The chime on the door alerted them of a new customer. The morning was dead thanks to everyone being at church. It gave them a quiet reprieve until now. James looked at Eli and nodded in silence as he moved through the door of the stockroom to the storefront.

"Eli, dad's back," James called out.

Eli rushed through a maze of shelves to stand beside James, waiting with curiosity to hear his dad's report. "What's the word? Did you find Lance?"

The eldest Bennet nodded and pulled out a stool positioned under the checkout counter, and slumped down. "We found Lance. He and Ed are on the way home now."

"Is he okay?" James asked.

"As okay as any young adult making a rash and terrible decision would be," Henry said.

"And what of the tape?" Eli jumped in.

"It's destroyed."

"But how do you know? How do you know it was the actual tape and not just a dummy?"

"Eli, please give me some modicum of credit. We received word of the location of both him and the tape. Lance verified it was the tape, and we set fire to it in the back parking lot of the motel he was staying in."

"So, it's done then. We'll be okay?" James asked.

"I think so."

"And what of Gianna? She can't just come in like a wrecking ball and get away scot-free."

"Eli, in life, you need to pick your battles lest you allow yourself to be drained completely. Gianna knows we all know what she is. I suspect we'll see neither hide nor hair of her again."

"But that's not good enough," Eli cried out.

Mr. Bennet reached over and put his hand on Eli's shoulder, giving it a squeeze. "Let it go, son." He looked at James. "Thank you for taking over the store while I was away. You've done an excellent job. It might be time to pass the torch."

James chuckled. "So you heading home now to tell mom?"

"I thought we could just close up the shop today and all have the day off."

"Well, we've had no customers yet and Eli is only in the back doing inventory," James said, looking at Eli.

"Only? Listen, it's riveting work. I'm having all the fun in the world organizing and counting screws, bolts, nails, washers, and nuts," Eli said, rolling his eyes.

"I'll see you boys at home," Henry said, getting up from the stool and pushing it back under the counter. "I'm off to go handle your mother," he paused, looking up to the ceiling, "Lord, give me strength."

James and Eli burst into laughter, dispersing, and began closing duties. Eli went to lock the doors behind his dad and turned the open sign around. James set to counting the register. Lightness enveloped them both. Each knew the "what could have beens" and the struggle to overcome had it come to pass. Whatever force allowed Lance to be found, Eli was grateful. Maybe there was still a sliver of hope that he'd keep his job and friendship with Darci.

They'd almost finished the tasks at hand when a small rap on the glass door made them look over. James' mouth fell open, and he froze. Eli looked at his brother and back at the door.

"I guess I'll let her in?" Eli waited for a reply. When James said nothing, he grabbed the keys off the counter, walked to the door, and opened it. "Long time no see." Charleigh grinned nervously. "James, I could use some fresh air, so I'll just walk home. You've got the rest of this, right?"

"Yeah, yeah, I got it," James stammered out.

"Cool, see you at home," Eli said, slinking past Charleigh as she took the door in her hand and walked through at the same time.

"The fuck is happening," Eli muttered to himself as he strode down the street towards their house.

Questions plagued Eli. It made zero sense that they could find Lance in a city as big as Dallas, with all its nooks and crannies. There was more to the story, and Eli needed to know every detail. He chuckled to himself. His mind was always in journalist mode, needing to know how all the threads tied together and find the loose one somewhere.

He turned onto their street and saw Marina climbing out of her silver rental car. "Marina," Eli called out. "Hey, before you go in, can we talk?"

"Sure," she said, closing the car door and leaning against it. "What do you want to talk about?"

"Lance."

"What about Lance? He should be here in the next few hours. Ed sent your dad ahead so he could fill in your mom."

Eli nodded. "It doesn't make sense."

"What?"

"How were they able to find Lance in a city with over a million people?"

Marina looked down at her feet and didn't answer.

"Marina, tell me."

"Those involved were told to omit the details of how they found him."

"I understand that," Eli said. "Add me to the list of secret keepers. I won't say anything to anyone."

Marina sighed. "Your dad and uncle had given up. Their efforts were fruitless until they received a visitor at their hotel room."

"A visitor?"

"Yes. Darci showed up, worse for the wear from what I was told, and gave them an address and made them swear not to mention her involvement."

"Darci," Eli repeated. Her name was one he'd not have ever expected to hear, especially in an affair such as this. It was below her and affected none of her kin. She'd left his apartment so abruptly. "You said she was worse for the wear?"

"Edward told me she smelled like a bar, her hair and clothes disheveled, and hands bloodied and swollen. They offered for her to go in and get cleaned up, but she refused, saying she had other matters to tend to."

"Holy hell," Eli said.

"Yeah," Marina said. "Don't tell anyone I told you. I'll never hear the end of it."

"My lips are sealed. Thank you for telling me."

"You're welcome," Marina said, pushing off the car door. "Now, let's go in and help your father with your mom, shall we?"

Chapter 32

M onths blurred by. Lance was home and processing how close
he came to taking the entire family out. James and Charleigh
seemed to have mended bridges and were inseparable. She'd a natural
knack for making people feel seen and heard at the store, which trans-
lated to more business. It warmed his heart to see James had found his
other half in life. Someone who would balance, support, and challenge
him. To think they'd met almost a year ago, and they found their way
back to each other, made him grin.

Eli shoved his hands in his jeans pockets as he walked through
the open field. Everyone's life seemed to either be back to normal
or improved. While he was happy for all of them, he struggled with
feeling envious. De Bourgh hadn't even called him to inquire if he
would come back or not. His conversations with Chase did little to
help, either. His life in the last year had become so messy it derailed all
of his ambitions. If he was being honest with himself, he didn't even
know if he still wanted a journalism career.

His decision to come back home seemed to be the most logical one. It'd allowed him to sort through his feelings and reevaluate what he wanted out of life. Daily walks became a routine, and he noticed he felt more alive and peaceful during them. When he would close his eyes, mental pictures of Pemberley's gardens would float to the surface. Not far behind were images of Darci, relaxed and free.

He came to the road across from his street. A black sedan with dark tinted windows pulled up, parking where he stood. The back window slowly rolled down, exposing its occupant.

"Get in," Keats said.

Eli looked each way before he walked around to the other side of the car, opened the door and slid in. He'd barely shut the door when the car peeled out and turned down main street.

"Where are we going?" Eli asked.

"Are you in a relationship with my niece?" Keats inquired point blank.

"Excuse me?"

"You heard me, Ellington Bennet. Are you in a relationship with my niece, Darci?"

Astonishment at the line of questions played out on his face. He'd assumed Keats was there to discuss his abrupt departure from De Bourgh, not this. This was entirely out of left field. "No, Keats, I'm not."

Keats nodded, his haughty demeanor thawing slightly. "And you will promise me you'll never enter a relationship with Darci?"

A laugh escaped from Eli. "I won't promise that."

"And why not?"

"Yes, 'why not' is the question, isn't it? Why not me and Darci? Would that be so wrong?"

"You must be joking. She is too good for you. You're of the wrong pedigree for her."

"Pedigree? Oh, you mean raised knowing the value of hard work, sacrifice and nothing being handed to me," Eli bit out.

"Darci is intended for my Andrew. Her mother wanted it to happen before she died."

"Does she know this?"

"Of course she does!" Keats spit out.

"Well, my condolences to Andrew and yourself. Now, if you wouldn't mind having your driver pull over to let me out."

"Do it, Greg."

The car slowed to a stop, pulling up to a curb. Eli opened the door, bending down to glare at Keats. "You can count this as my two weeks' notice," he said before he slammed the car door shut and turned to start his trek back home.

It had been only five minutes since walking through the door that Kit accosted him, bouncing up and down in excitement. "Did you hear?"

"Kit, I literally just got here. No, I've not heard anything."

"We've been invited to a picnic today at Netherfield Park! Mom suspects James will propose to Charleigh today, too!"

Mark chose that moment to throw down his two cents as he walked to Kit. "It's not even been a full year since they met. If you ask me, it's a mistake. They're just living in a fictitious world filled with warm fuzzies and nothing else."

"It's close enough to a year. Why do you always have to bring the mood down, Mark?" Kit spat out.

"I'm sorry my being a realist has thwarted your idealistic joy," Mark retorted.

Eli pushed past Kit and Mark, walking up the stairs. James' bedroom door was slightly ajar. He knocked on the door frame. "James, can I come in?"

A muffled "Yeah" came from the room. Eli pushed the door open and saw James in the closet, digging through things and throwing them every which way.

"What are you doing?"

"Ah ha! Found it," James said as he turned to leave his closet, a small ring box firmly planted in his hand.

"So, mom's right. You plan to ask Charleigh to marry you?"

"I think so, yes," James said nervously.

"When did you get the ring?"

James grinned sheepishly. "After my accident at Charleigh's, I decided I'd like to spend the rest of my life with her, if you remember."

"I remember. James, why didn't you tell me? I knew her leaving was hard, but I'd not realized how much of a struggle it was for you."

"You had your own issues," James said, looking at Eli. "It's okay, though. I know you'd have dropped everything to be with me, which is why I said nothing."

Eli walked over and wrapped James in a tight hug before stepping back and placing his hands on either shoulder. "Well, I'm beyond happy for you. Do you need any help with sorting out your proposal plans?" Eli chuckled. "Shall I run interference on mom and Kit?"

"I think I'll be okay. Besides, she knows how our family is," James said with a laugh.

"Show me this ring."

James held out the box, pulling it open. A thin white gold band gleamed. The small princess cut diamond centered in the middle shimmered. It was nothing extravagant. The simplicity of it spoke to their relationship. From their first meeting at the Netherfield party, they only had eyes for each other. Status had fallen to the wayside, allowing unconditional love to blossom and grow.

"It's perfect, James."

Chapter 33

Vibrant colors painted the fields surrounding Netherfield. The light blue sky highlighted the landscape and house. Mother Nature seemed to have painted it solely for James and Charleigh. They pulled into the drive and parked. Rose bushes created a hedge row, all in full bloom with reds, yellows, pinks, and whites. Eli smiled. This house was the outside representation of Charleigh's personality, light and happy.

The front door opened and Charleigh walked out, a radiant smile plastered on her face. Her white floral print sundress fluttered in the breeze as she walked down the steps to meet them. She looked at the window, making eye contact with James, and bounced up and down, impatiently waiting for everyone to unload. She ran the moment James exited, jumped up, and wrapped her legs around his waist, her arms clutching his neck. James held her in his arms and hugged her to him.

There were only two of them at that moment. Love poured from both. Giggles and laughs cascaded from Charleigh as James whispered in her ear. She leaned back, adoringly nodding, placing her hands on either side of his cheeks, and gave him a deep and passionate kiss. James set her down, pulled out the little black box, and opened it. Charleigh's hands flew to her chest, tears streamed down her face. He pulled the ring out of its home, placed the box back in his pocket, and reached out for her hand.

Eli's heart felt full as he watched the ring slide upon Charleigh's finger. For how much they'd both been through, this was the ending he'd hoped they'd have. Every ounce of this forever love was well-deserved. If only more in the world could see past differences of the heart in those that surrounded them. He looked around at his family. While they were a baffling mess, they each held their own place in making the dynamic what it was.

Kit, the hopeless romantic, hugged their sobbing matriarch. Mark, a beacon of all that was moral and right, leaned against the van, his arms crossed. Lance, the impetuous risk-taker, stood by their father. The grays seemed more pronounced in his dad's hair and lines deeper than they were before. However, the crinkle around his eyes shone pride.

James took Charleigh's hand, and she led them around the back of the house. In the center of the garden stood a white tent with a couple of round tables and chairs underneath its canopy. Each table held trays of finger foods and plates with pink pastel folded napkins lining the outer edges. Kit and Lance ran ahead and pulled out chairs, plopped down, and removed the napkins. Mark trudged, taking a seat next to Kit, looking over at the both of his siblings with a critical eye. Henry walked over to the table, pulled out a chair for his wife, and let her settle in before sitting next to her.

Eli looked at the wood line. Everything had fallen into place for those he loved. He put his hands in his pockets and strolled towards the comfort of the forest. His soul needed to get lost for a bit. There was still so much to figure out in his own life. It was an odd feeling, being directionless. He always had a plan, and it was unsettling to not know what the future held.

He found a large moss covered tree stump and sat. His eyes settled on the horses that roamed freely. Twigs broke underneath the feet of an intruder. Eli looked back. A soft blue spaghetti strapped ankle length dress caught his eye. Her loose, up swept brunette hair was no match for the near constant whiffs of warm air. Tendrils of hair flitted across her freckled face. Unspoken words passed between the two. Eli gave a slow nod, watching as she made her way to the stump and sat next to him.

"Hi."

"Hi," Darci said, looking down at her intertwined fingers. "I'm sorry."

"I'm sorry, too."

"You've nothing to be sorry about, Eli. Every step of the way, I've been the one to make a mess of things."

"You can hardly take all that on," Eli said. "I'm just as guilty. I judged you without even knowing you." Eli sighed while focusing on a painted horse in the field. "I've done you a disservice. I even agreed to destroy your career and family's company."

"I know." Darci sat quietly for a time and nodded.

"So, who did you punch?" Eli asked.

"How did you know I punched someone?" Darci asked, her eyes widening.

"I'm a journalist, Darci," Eli chuckled.

"A good one at that," Darci laughed. "I'm not proud of it," she said, "but Gianna. She's had it coming."

"Thank you for coming to my family's aid."

"Oh," Darci said, biting her lower lip. "It's what you do when you care about someone." Eli turned to look at her, holding her gaze. "My feelings towards you haven't changed, Eli. They've only gotten stronger." She sighed. "I know I'm completely unworthy and understand if you still feel the same about me as you did months ago."

Eli reached out and enveloped her hands in his. "Darci," he said, moving a hand up to wipe a tear that fell down her cheek. "These last couple months, since walking the grounds of Pemberley, have been the most aimless of my life. My heart is undone. It tore me to pieces knowing I'd only just realized my affections for you and then lost my chance." Eli pushed a loose strand of hair behind her ear. "Forever I'm yours, Darci Williams."

Darci burst into tears, her breath hitching. The dam had broken. "Eli, I love you."

"I love you, too," Eli said, wiping the tears from her face with his thumbs. "May I kiss you?"

At her nod, Eli scooted closer to Darci and ran his fingers into her hair, cradling her as he brought his lips to hers. Salty sweetness danced upon his tongue as she opened her lips to receive him. Warmth rushed through him, comforting his restless heart. This was where he needed to be, by her side. They were equals in every sense of the word.

I remember going to my grandparent's house every other weekend to visit them from my childhood to teenage years. My grandmother is a retired elementary school teacher and my grandfather was a college professor once he retired as a Colonel from the Air Force. Even now, I think back to the legacies they both gave me. Their love of books and t.v./movie adaptations of classical literature pieces is burrowed deep within my heart.

When I close my eyes and remember, I see them both in their matching tan recliners, gently rocking and a glass table with a tall lamp attached, settled between them. I'd hear the sounds of one of the many brilliantly done VHS tapes, they'd pulled from their Tower of London tape stand, and would pad my way over the soft cream-colored carpet to their room, peek my head around, and ask if I could watch too. They always greeted me with a smile and a nod. Camping out on their bedroom floor, watching the likes of Little Women, Anne of Green Gables, and yes, Pride & Prejudice gave me a sense of belonging I'd yearned for.

Tears well-up in my eyes every time I think back to them. Hearing my grandfather chuckle at the wittiness of Mr. Bennet and the sheer ridiculousness of Mr. Collins, warmed my heart. They both swore by the BBC tv movie series as the best version, because of its in-depth exploration of characters rather than just focusing on the major events. And after watching countless remakes myself, I must agree with them outside of one pivotal creative genius that is Lost in Austen.

My love for Jane Austen's stylistic writing and her linguistics grew as I got older and understood why my grandparents loved her works. Jane, through her own lived experiences, fought back against the norms of her time, highlighting the inauspiciousness and absurdity of the world for women of the time. She used her poignant words subversively, pushing back against society and challenged those who read her works to look in a mirror.

In Jane's most famous line opening of a literary work, "It is a truth universally acknowledged, that a single man in possession of a good fortune, must be in want of a wife", she eloquently slams 'the universal truth' because it isn't an *actual* truth rather the subjective *must* that dictated behaviors of men and women. Everyone of her main female characters pushes the envelope, fighting against marrying just as a means to an end. It is love that ultimately wins out, regardless of circumstances of birth, upbringing, connections, etcetera.

It was a man's literary world, though you had brilliant feminist minds refusing to being viewed as mere proliferations of family lines. They argued through their writing that women had every ability to love, think for themselves, feel all emotions, and had the power to live their lives on their own terms. Jane Austen did so herself, never marrying, after the love of her life passed away. Jane was a strong heroine of her own story and lived how she wrote her heroines to be.

It is with all of that in mind that I decided it was time to write a modern-dayish variation of one of her famous works that would actually represent the world as it is and celebrate her work written 211 years ago on this day. I'm tired of only reading and seeing adaptations with only cis hetero white cast members, especially since I've got children who identify as part of the LGBTQIA+ community. Seeing them represented in literature and media matters to me. As a white cis hetero female, those aren't my stories to tell. However, I can show my support by incorporating characters who are part of the community and share the history. As Jane was one of the first of her time to write pieces bucking the system, I think she'd have been one of the first to retell her own work to represent the ever changing societal and political climate, and push for change via self-reflection through reading. My gratitude for what my grandparents gave to me, and what Jane gave the world, is forever expanding as I grow in wisdom and understanding each day.

None of this would be possible if I didn't have my husband pushing me, supporting me and all my various side quests, and sometimes kicking me in the proverbial butt to drink water, eat, write, and take care of me. I lucked out in marrying my best friend. Thank you, love, for everything you've done, continue to do, and will do. I can't imagine doing life with anyone else.

To my children, thank you for being you. We each are perfectly imperfect, which is what makes life with you all beautiful. I can firmly say that you all have taught me more than I could ever teach you. You all make me so proud. I've felt every up and down and am grateful for our close relationship, mutual respect and trust. I love you all so much. You're one of my favorites.

While this inclusive story idea was 'done' in my mind, I'm so thankful for the guidance of Aiden Siobhan of Laura Dail Literary Agency, author Jayne Allen, and author Rebecca Balcárcel, who were speakers at DFW Con 2023 via a Diversity & Representation panel. Once I talked to them, I quickly realized this piece wasn't finished, and that there were aspects regarding Chase's character and story that needed to be explored. I walked away with clarity, understanding, and direction on how to better represent the marginalized communities within these pages.

Special thanks go to Morri, who beta and sensitivity read the revamped manuscript after I had worked to give Chase more layers. Thank you for giving of your time and being open and honest with me. I appreciate it beyond measure.

Vicky and Lisa, you guys are rock stars and two people I am so lucky to have cheering me on.

Last but not at all least, thank you, Kimber, for knowing how to point my flame-throwing chaos self in a positive direction. Your friendship is unparalleled and a genuine treasure. The fact you let me run amok with business card trading and rainbow vomiting about your books while under the influence of I don't know how many hurricanes (Thanks Mr. Kimber for instigating all of that) and humoring me by letting me think I talked/dragged you into buying DFW Con tickets, driving a billion hours to come with me to DFW Con, and forcing your hand in picture appointments and conversing. I can't imagine my life without you in it. Thank you for your constant support, butt kicks, laughing with and at me, sharing in my downs, and taking over as my editor of all things. And no, reader, you can't have Kimber. She's mine. Go find your own. Also, I'm sorry for any for any mistakes in the acknowledgments, but I couldn't very well send it to you to edit and ruin the fun could I?

Also by the Author

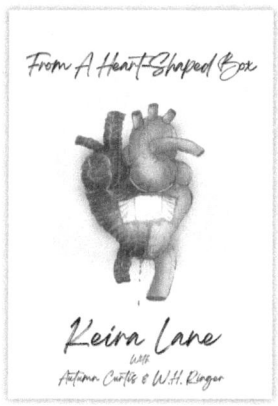

From A Heart-Shaped Box is a collection of nine short stories focusing on various forms of love, with the finale being the novella Oath Breaker. Within the book are stories of metamorphosis, brokenness, loss, sacrifice, inner strength, retribution, and much more!

Though the stories within From A Heart-Shaped Box are works of fiction, it captures raw sentiment and shares it with the reader to let them know that while life experiences differ, emotions don't, and we are truly never alone.

About the Author

Hailing from West Texas, Keira grew up the oldest of five siblings. Her grandmother introduced her to the works of Jane Austen at a young age, which sparked her love affair with books and writing. As a budding author, with her debut From A Heart-Shaped Box released November 2020, Keira has shown that sheer determination and resilience are keys to growing in the literary arts.

Fueled by coffee and neurodiverse chaos, Keira has managed to not only get published in two books, she was featured in The Dark Side of Purity Vol III zine and co-founded Autimagination Media, a media outlet that specializes in podcasts that uplift various social causes, all in less than three years.

Keira lives in Fort Worth, Texas with her husband, five neurodiverse children, some of whom identify as members to the LGBTQIA+ community, two dogs, and three cats. When she's not squirreling and trying to stick her hands in all the cookie jars, Keira enjoys reading books of all different genres, writing, photography, painting, crafts, hanging with her family, playing video games, potatoes and Moscato.

www.ingramcontent.com/pod-product-compliance
Lightning Source LLC
Chambersburg PA
CBHW050737180626
46814CB00002B/802